FROZEN LIES

By
R. A. Quinn

(A Jacob Rohn Novel - Volume l)
3rd Edition

Frozen Lies

Published by:
Tier 1 Books
Pueblo, Colorado 81006
www.tier1books.com

Revised 10/14/13

eBook version also available
from Amazon and Barnes & Noble

Print version ISBN numbers:
ISBN-13: 978-0-9897332-1-2
ISBN-10: 0989733211

Table of Contents

Dedication

For T - my wife and best friend.
Thank you for all your encouragement (nagging & complaining) and many years of support (telling me what to do).

Acknowledgements

There are many who deserve to be listed here, where would I even begin? For everyone who has believed in me, given me a chance or stood up for me – thank you. I certainly want to thank my family that has always been there for me when I needed it the most – you know who you are.

Prologue

He woke up and rolled over to see the red digits of the alarm clock on the nightstand next to his bed. The bright numbers read three-thirty a.m., two hours before he was due to rise for the day. *"Damn,"* he thought. *"Three-thirty in the morning is way too early for me."*

Was it the pain in his knee? Was it something stirring inside the house? What caused him to wake up in the middle of the night for at least the hundredth time over the last few months?

Wishing he could go back to sleep, he lay there and listened to the steady breathing of man's best friend who was asleep on the oval rug at the foot of the bed. That certainly ruled out an intruder of some sort. Archie would have alerted him to the presence of anything inside or outside of their home. His mind wandered back to thoughts of playing fetch with his faithful mutt. He still felt the soreness in his right arm and shoulder from tossing a tennis ball across the yard for Archie to chase, catch and return to him to toss again.

Archie was a Black Lab male who adopted him four years earlier. He arrived home one spring afternoon to discover the Lab puppy curled up on the porch as if that was the Lab's home and he was waiting for his human to let him inside. He spent days asking around trying to find out who was the puppy's owner. An ad was placed in the newspaper, on craigslist, as well as on some local bulletin boards. He checked at the local animal shelter for several weeks but no clue was revealed as to the identity of the puppy's original owner. It remained an unsolved mystery. Weeks turned into months and then into years. Archie was there to stay; there was no denying that fact. He always looked at it as though Archie was his own dog who was just passing through but had decided he found a great place to stay where all of his needs would be taken care of without question. Not that it was a bad thing. Caring for a dog had made the past few years much easier to deal with. Archie had certainly been a great companion.

A new companion hadn't been the only change in his life. His career had taken a new direction; he had come to a new area and was finally on a solid path once again. Archie turned into a true friend who never questioned what he was thinking, what he was doing, or what his motives were, nor did he make a fuss about socks left on the floor.

He rolled over and once again looked at the clock, four-o-five a.m. He recalled a time long ago when he was jarred from sleep at four-o-five a.m. Why couldn't he get that thought out of his memory? Was it possible to get that time removed from all clocks so that he would never have to see it again?

He considered taking an early morning run but discarded that idea since he knew the temperature to be below freezing. Maybe an early shower and settling in with a book would be a good way to kill some time. "Can't I just go back to sleep for heaven's sake?" he muttered.

He closed his eyes for a moment but was startled by the ringing of the telephone. He fumbled for the phone on the nightstand next to the clock. There were those big red numbers shining in his eyes and mocking him, four-o-five a.m. *"Where's that damn phone?"* he wondered. Even though the phone had been in the same place for almost five years, he wasn't able to find it. It seemed to be ringing louder and louder but he couldn't locate and answer it so that friggin' thing would stop that infernal racket. *"Where in the hell is that damn phone?"* he thought. It was definitely not where it should be. *"Who in the hell is calling so early in the morning anyway?"* It was frustrating to hear it; he knew where it was but was unable to answer the god-forsaken thing. *"Shit, who would be calling at this hour?"* Why couldn't he find it?

He decided to get up and turn on the light so that he could find the phone but as he did so, he stumbled forward. *"What the hell?"* was his immediate thought. The phone cord was wrapped around his legs and he vaulted forward. He prepared himself for a hard impact as he expected to hit the floor but instead he just kept falling.

As quickly as it began, the ringing of the phone stopped and was replaced by the repetitive beeping of the alarm. His eyes flew open. The big red numbers on the clock now read five-thirty a.m. He closed his eyes tightly against the harsh red glow, then reached over and turned off the alarm. Another dream; the same damn nightmare. "Dammit!" he softly exclaimed. He knew it was going to be a long day. Time to get his ass perpendicular and get moving; Archie needed to go outside. He braced himself for the difficult day ahead as his feet hit the cold floor.

Chapter 1

I listened to the hum of the snowmachine's engine as I glided along the worn trail. I grew up calling these machines snowmobiles. I called them a snowmobile only once after I moved to Anchorage and was immediately chastised by a lifelong Alaskan. Most locals called them snowmachines or sleds, but there were some that preferred the term *'snogo'*. The way the trail was packed down, it was apparent that many snowmachines had taken that same trail throughout the winter.

That far north, even in mid-March it was ten degrees below zero. The sky was a beautiful blue without a cloud in sight. The sharp, clear cold air almost seemed to have its own color. If it didn't, then it should have. I'm not sure what you would call the color of cold air but it damn sure was an amazing sight to behold. There was no smog from industry or cars to desecrate the wild beauty that was before me. Simply put, it was an amazingly crystal clear day.

It was mid-afternoon and since the days were getting longer that time of year, several hours of daylight remained before nightfall.

There was no need to hurry as I had only a few miles to go, and so I could just enjoy the moment. Few people ever witnessed such extreme wilderness and raw beauty. The snow cover was at least three feet deep but the beaten down trail was easily navigated by my iron horse of the Arctic. The willow bushes were frosted over and the spruce trees were holding a blanket of snow on their dark green branches. All around me was scenery you would expect to see in an art gallery, lining the walls for all to behold and enjoy.

I had seen ptarmigan by the dozens. These beautiful white birds, about the size of a partridge, were abundant in the north. At times you would observe a willow and think its branches were dotted with tuffs of snow. All at once, what you thought had been snow would burst into flight as the ptarmigan would glide across the tops of the willows in their escape from perceived danger. Rabbits had been darting across my trail all day long. Wildlife was abundant with the occasional sighting of fox and moose.

"Jacob Rohn, you have it made," I silently reflected.

It was a picture perfect day north of the Arctic Circle just a few miles outside of Fort Yukon, Alaska. As I exhaled, my breath resembled small puffs of fog that hung suspended in front of my face only to disappear and then reappear moments later. Frost had built up on the outer edges of my parka hood, mostly on the fur ruff that encircled my face. I wore a full face gaiter that also had frost around the mouth and nose openings. There was no doubt that I resembled an abominable snowman, if such a creature even existed. The trail that I followed turned and approached the Porcupine River which was just a few miles from my final destination of the day.

The land along the Porcupine River was typically flat in the Fort Yukon area with both tundra and tree growth. The heaviest stands of trees were along the river or around lakes, meadows and sloughs. The farther away from the river corridor you traveled, the fewer trees you would encounter. What I saw the most were spruce and willows with an occasional birch tree.

I focused my mind and thought about the day so far. I caught an early flight out of Anchorage to arrive in Fairbanks at eight-thirty that morning. Then a commuter flight put me into Fort Yukon by ten-fifteen a.m. Settled just above the Arctic Circle, Fort Yukon had a year round population of perhaps six-hundred residents who lived varying lifestyles. I had hoped to meet with the Chief of Police of this tiny community located along the banks of the Yukon River about one-hundred-fifty miles northeast of Fairbanks. The Chief would be busy working on a case for a few hours according to the text message he sent me. No problem, I could always meet with him later in the day.

My move to Alaska occurred five years earlier. I grew up in Florida and had enlisted for a three year stretch in the army after finishing high school. After I ended my military tour, I moved to Colorado Springs, Colorado, for no particular reason other than I had a good friend in the military who was from there and that was all he talked about. Without realizing it, my friend had convinced me into moving there. It was sad that he never knew this since he was killed in a training accident before completing his tour of military duty.

At the age of twenty-two I had been accepted to the police academy and was hired by the Colorado Springs police department after completing my training. I was promoted to detective after about six years and was very happy with my chosen profession. Though I never married, I was engaged for a time. The engagement had ended unexpectedly and I felt a change was in order. That happened to be in the very same year that I turned thirty years old.

I learned that Alaska was forming a special unit of about ten investigators that would work out of an office under the direction of the State Attorney General that would provide support or conduct criminal investigations on all levels throughout Alaska. The investigators would also be tasked with assisting in training police across the state. In Alaska, the Attorney General was the chief legal advisor to the state government. The idea to have a team of investigators under that office was to create a buffer from normal political interference. At least that was how it was explained to me.

I applied for one of the positions and after a lengthy process I was hired so I moved to the largest and coldest state in the nation. Five years later the unit had dwindled down to just five active investigators and one supervisor, as a result of budget cuts.

Everyone in the unit lived in Anchorage and we all were fortunate enough to have the opportunity to travel and assist with or investigate high profile cases all around the state. Usually we were accepted by all law enforcement agencies in Alaska, but occasionally, when we were directed to work with or take over investigations from the state boys, they frowned upon us being there, but it always worked out.

Fort Yukon served as a hub for numerous villages in the Yukon Flats area. The people of that town were from a variety of ethnic backgrounds but were predominantly Alaska Natives. The closest village was about twenty miles away, but there were no roads to that village. A regional medical clinic, school district, post office and Federal Bureau of Land Management, as well as numerous state offices were based in Fort Yukon to provide services to its residents and to the region.

Gwicyaa Zhee, or *'house on the flats'* as it was called by the Gwich'in speaking inhabitants, was first established in the mid 1800s by the Hudson Bay Company as a trading post. Fort Yukon was officially incorporated in 1959, the year Alaska became the forty-ninth state.

Fort Yukon was quite isolated but was accessible by air all year round. You could get there by boat from a couple of different directions during the warmer months when the river was ice free. If you were hardy enough you could reach the town by snowmachine in the winter. The community wasn't on the road system, meaning that there were no roadways that connected it to any other community in the entire state.

After an early lunch at the local restaurant I prepared for the ten mile snowmachine journey east of town. Since officially I worked for the State of Alaska, I had snowmachines available to me which were stored by the State Fish and Game department in Fort Yukon. The large sleds were housed in a heated shop and were maintained very well by the crews who spent much of their time collecting data on the winter moose population in the region. I happened to be there at a time when they weren't.

Before I left work on Friday my boss had outlined my assignment for this trip: travel to Fort Yukon and return to the scene of a horrific murder/suicide that had happened the previous November. A young Canadian couple, Jess and Linda Crane, had been living at a caretaker's cabin near a local lodge. Big Moose Lodge was located along the Porcupine River ten miles from town. The couple had come to the area the previous May and worked for the lodge owners and were to be the caretakers for the lodge over the winter months.

During the late spring and summer months, guests flocked to the lodge for fishing, hunting and sightseeing adventures. The lodge closed each year for the winter in mid-October. The Cranes had taken the job which consisted of housekeeping and basic maintenance during the months when the guests were present and general caretaker duties once the lodge closed for the season.

After the lodge closed in mid-October, the young couple took over the duties of watching over the lodge for the winter.

In early November, a grisly discovery was made at the Cranes' cabin. A local resident was returning from running his trap-line. He decided to stop at the Big Moose Lodge caretaker's cabin for a quick rest and maybe to have a cup of coffee.

The door to the cabin was secured from the inside and no one responded to a knock. From all appearances, including the snowmachine the Cranes used being parked in front of the cabin, someone should have been there but there was no smoke from the stove pipe that extended from the roof of the cabin. The trapper peered through the front window and was able to see the obviously deceased bodies of the couple inside the structure.

An investigation concluded that Crane had shot his wife and then himself. The door was secured from the inside and there was no sign of any burglary or struggle. The murder weapon was where you would expect it to be found in that type of case. I hadn't been part of the original investigation but was merely returning to the scene at the request of the State Attorney's office in Anchorage to take one final look at the case before it was closed for good. My job was to ensure that the current conclusion was accurate and the case could, in fact, be closed as a murder/suicide. I would put it in the category of just making sure everything was as it seemed to be. After all, the lodge would open in a little over a month and the crime scene hadn't been formally released back to the owners.

I had read over the case file for the third time while traveling to Fort Yukon earlier that day. Everything seemed straight forward and in order. The Cranes had no known enemies and though there were a few reports obtained from the local PD of some domestic disputes between the couple, there had been no real violence or arrests. The couple came from Canada, their families were from Canada and they all were average people. They had no known connections to anything dishonest or dangerous. The investigation pointed toward an episode of *'cabin fever'* as it's referred to when a person or group of people have been isolated in a small space and have a claustrophobic reaction. It's believed something must have snapped with Jess Crane, who shot his wife dead, and then turned the gun on himself. Everything seemed to fit with the original investigation and findings, from what I could tell. That was my task, to ensure that the report, notes and investigation fit the scene and the current conclusion and then report my findings back to my supervisor. An easy and straight forward assignment.

Chapter 2

My time at the caretaker's cabin was uneventful. The cabin itself was a log structure about twenty feet by twenty feet in size. One window and door were to the front of the cabin. A single smoke stack protruded from the tin roof. The cabin had one small room that was used as a bedroom and a smaller second room which was used as a wash room and storage area. The remainder of the cabin was open with a wood stove which was used for cooking and heating and was the main focus of the room. A set of cabinets and wash basin were to the left of the wood stove. A wooden table separated the kitchen and the remainder of the living space. A couch and a small desk completed the meager furnishings in the cabin.

The fixtures inside the cabin were definitely sparse. It was evident that the Cranes hadn't lived there all that long as it didn't have a warm homey feel. Perhaps it was that they hadn't lived there long enough to do much decorating, or just didn't possess the money, or have enough time to add much in the way of personal touches. Either way, the place resembled a cabin you would rent for a weekend and to which you just brought a few personal items with you in order to get by with for a short time.

The scene description, as well as the diagrams and photos, all seemed to fit the obvious conclusion. Try as I might, I couldn't come up with a scenario that would have the case play out as something other than a murder/suicide. Even after spending the better part of two hours scrutinizing the scene and checking it against what was in the file, nothing seemed irregular or out of place.

I was on the last leg of my trip back to Fort Yukon. As I continued to enjoy the beautiful scenery, I imagined what it would have been like to settle such harsh country fifty years ago or more. It's untamed now; it had to be relentless all those years ago. The people who braved such unforgiving land were special indeed, and still were in my opinion.

As I approached the last meadow I would cross before getting to town, I stopped my machine at the edge of the clearing which stretched out for about a hundred yards in front of me and was about fifty yards wide. I cut off the engine and listened to the wonderful quiet as I sat there on my machine. The peacefulness that surrounded me was the only thing that rivaled the clear skies and beautiful scenery. The trail I followed dissected the meadow perfectly. The snow was mostly undisturbed on either side of the trail with the exception of a few rabbit and fox tracks that branched off in different directions. Spruce trees with an occasional birch tree surrounded the meadow.

The scenery was utterly gorgeous and I had a front row seat. I removed my gloves to pull my digital camera from an inside pocket under my bulky parka. The meadow was a place of beauty that I wanted to capture in a photo. I snapped a picture as a raven glided across my field of view. It was a great shot and I was proud as I reviewed my work on the tiny LCD screen on the back of the camera.

I tugged at my heavy parka and put the camera back into the inside pocket. In these temperatures it was best to keep the camera as close to my body heat as possible to help maintain proper functioning and to extend the life of the battery. As I donned my gloves, I dropped one glove next to my right foot. Just as I leaned over to the right to retrieve my glove, I heard the sharp crack of a high powered rifle. The report of the firearm had broken the peaceful silence for an instant. The silence returned just as quickly but seemed even more intense. I had no idea where the shot originated or what its designed target had been.

Was there a hunter in the area? I hadn't heard or seen anyone since I left town more than three hours ago. I remained low and slid to the right side of the snowmachine as I grasped the grips of the forty caliber Smith and Wesson handgun that was secured in a shoulder holster under my left arm. It was no quick draw but within a couple of seconds I had the gun in my right hand and listened intently for any sound or clue as to where that shot had been fired. I glanced up at the windshield of my machine and there was a single, perfectly round hole about the size of my pinkie finger dead center of the plastic windshield - exactly where my body had been just an instant before I had leaned over to pick up my glove. At least now I knew what the bullet was intended to hit.

Knowing that I'd been the target of a sniper didn't make me feel any better. I made myself one with the ground and kept my body as close to and behind the frame and engine of my transportation as I possibly could.

I was considering my next move when I heard the engine of a snowmachine come to life and then roar away towards town, in the same direction I had been going. The get-away was within a minute of hearing the gunshot. Other than that, I heard nothing but silence.

I stayed put for a couple of minutes longer but all that I heard was the sound of my heart pounding inside my chest and dead silence all around me. I wasn't so sure which was the loudest. Without a better plan, I scrambled to my feet and straddled my machine. A quick pull of the rope start and the engine of my snowmachine started up. A strong squeeze of the throttle caused my machine to lurch forward and like a rocket, I took off towards town, which was perhaps a mile away. As I finished crossing the meadow and pulled into the trees I came upon the clear tracks of a snowmachine that had been stopped on the trail and there were some boot impressions next to those tracks.

The spot had been chosen perfectly as there was a clear view of the meadow from the direction I was traveling but was fairly concealed from the place where I had dropped my glove, due to some low brush. The tracks indicated that a single person had been traveling the trail I was on and had stopped their machine there in anticipation of seeing a rider on the same trail across the meadow. That rider had to be me!

I snapped a few photos of the marks in the snow: the boot tracks and snowmachine tracks of the person I believed intended on shooting a large hole directly through me. The snow was soft and any impressions of tread patterns were not discernible. I believed the person was of average weight and perhaps wore a size eleven boot. That was about all I could tell from the mostly obliterated tracks. I was unable to locate a single scrap of evidence left behind by the unknown assailant, other than those indiscernible tracks.

I really had my list of suspects narrowed down to perhaps a person with about an eleven inch foot and probably average weight and who owned a hunting rifle. That pretty much included every adult in town.

Chapter 3

The remainder of my trip into town was uneventful. As I got closer, the trail branched off in several different directions. It had been quite some time since there had been any fresh snow. Snowmachines were a major source of winter transportation for everyone in the area, and there were so many tracks that it was impossible to follow those left by my assailant. I went directly to the PD, slid to a stop, then climbed off of my machine and went inside to meet the Chief.

The first person I saw was Fanny Grant. Fanny was a long time resident of Fort Yukon who served as the clerk and daytime dispatcher for the department. She always wore sleeveless dresses and had a sweater around her shoulders with only the top button fastened. She sported what I called big hair and normally a pencil was stuck in her hair above her right ear with the eraser sticking out toward the front. She had a pair of reading glasses hooked to a dainty gold chain around her neck. Yeah, Fanny was certainly stylish.

"You look as if you're enjoying your visit," Fanny chirped as I entered the office.

"You don't know the half of it Fanny," I told her.

"I heard from Alice at the post office that *'Jake Rohn'* was in town again. I was sort of put out that you didn't stop to see me earlier but then the Chief said you had business out by Big Moose Lodge," Fanny said. "Something about the Crane case I would imagine."

Apparently it was no secret that I flew in that morning. If Alice at the post office knew I presumed everyone did. I liked Fanny but I had many other things on my mind at the moment, so I got right to the point. "Is the Chief in?" I asked.

Fanny picked up her telephone handset and dialed the Chief's extension. She spoke into the handset and said I was waiting out front. Fanny returned the phone to its cradle. "Chief Sully will be right out."

Within seconds a hulking frame emerged through the door and Chief of Police Larry Sullivan stood in front of me. I had known the Chief since shortly after his arrival in Alaska. To his better friends he was known simply as Sully. Chief Sullivan looked as if he had just ridden in off the set of a B western movie. He had short black hair with a thick black moustache that I suspected he used hair coloring on in order to keep out the grey. He wore a sheepskin vest over a blue denim shirt and his blue jeans were held up with a heavy leather belt and big silver buckle. He always wore black boots to complete his outfit. Had he been outside, I knew he would be wearing a white cowboy hat.

"Well, you found your way there and back. I'm impressed, or did you make it back just to ask for directions?" Chief Sully said with a big grin.

"Very funny Sully. Can we talk in private for a few minutes?"

Sully, or Chief Sully as he was referred to by everyone in town, turned and motioned for me to follow. He walked back down the hall to his office and I followed. As we entered, he paused to let me pass and then shut the door behind us.

There was a chair in front of his desk, so I pulled it out and had a seat as Sully walked around the desk. I watched him and thought about when Chief Sullivan first came to Fort Yukon about three years earlier. He had been a deputy sheriff in Idaho for twenty-five years. That's why he looked like a misplaced cowboy all the time. He and his wife came to rural Alaska after their last child moved away from home. Claire, Sully's wife, was a teacher at the local grade school. She reminded me of Aunt Bee from Andy Griffith's fictional television town of Mayberry. These empty nesters were wonderful people in my opinion.

They both were well respected locally and among their professional colleagues, which was a difficult task for anyone in small town America. In rural Alaska, I thought it was even more difficult to accomplish that feat, if you asked me.

I first met Sully when we worked together on a major bootlegging case that was based in Fairbanks. Some residents of Fort Yukon had been used as runners to deliver alcohol to nearby dry villages. A dry village is one that had adopted a local option to ban the sale and possession of alcoholic beverages. The sale of a fifth of cheap vodka went as high as one-hundred-fifty dollars, or more at times.

Sully had different awards, accolades, thank you letters, pictures and other various forms of accomplishments covering the wall behind him. He was a well decorated cop. In our business we called that the *'I love me wall.'*

Sully sat down and looked at me from across his desk. "What's on your feeble?" he asked.

I guess he mistook my look of being shaken up from being shot at as misunderstanding his reference to my feeble mind.

"What is it you wanted to talk to me about?" Sully asked more directly.

"Who have you spoken with about my being here today?"

"Well, no one except for Fanny, who asked me because she heard you were in town from Alice at the post office. Fanny pretty much figured out you were here for the Crane case up at Big Moose Lodge. I ain't said anything about the reason you were here to anyone," Sully explained.

"Did you hear anyone else speak about me being here or ask you about me being in town?"

"No, what's with all these questions?"

"I think someone wants me dead for some reason."

I told Chief Sully about what happened on my way back into town, how I had almost been shot. I didn't say anything about my findings at the Cranes' cabin. I wanted to fish a little because Chief Sully might have heard something before now that could be important but not realize it at the moment. I wanted him to think naturally and not be swayed by anything I would say to him.

"That was a close call; I'm happy you're okay," he said. "I'm even happier I don't have to investigate a homicide scene outdoors in below zero weather." He paused as he realized that the dry cop humor wasn't working on me. "What's your first notion on why this happened?"

"I wish I knew. It most certainly has something to do with the Crane case itself. This case was all but closed as a murder/suicide and out of the blue I show up and head straight out to the crime scene. You were a big part of this investigation, so you tell me your gut feeling. Is there a chance that there's more to this than what meets the eye?"

Sully leaned forward with a thoughtful expression. "You know what; I felt something odd about this in the beginning but couldn't put my finger on it. I had expressed my thoughts to all the investigators who had any involvement in this case. I knew both of those kids for six months; they weren't perfect but I just couldn't believe that Crane would have shot his wife and then himself."

The Chief changed position in his chair and continued. "You've seen the file; there wasn't any evidence that could be found to prove that this was a double murder. There was no motive, evidence or anything else that could have even suggested or supported such a thought."

"Well, this case can be the only reason why anyone would have wanted me out of the picture," I responded. "Unless you know of something else going on here that I don't or haven't even considered."

"There's nothing happening right now," said Chief Sully. "I don't have any ongoing investigations or reports that would send up a red flag. The last thing out of the ordinary that we've had here was the Cranes' murder/suicide and now, this apparent attempt on your life. There aren't any strange people in town. The reason for this has me completely baffled."

My mind absorbed what Chief Sully had said. Right now I was tired and just wanted to relax a bit and think this through. I stood and extended my hand which Chief Sully accepted and shook.

"Chief, it's been a long day. I'm staying at the Fish and Game bunkhouse for the night and I'll review the Crane case file again as soon as I settle in. I need to check in with my office as well. My priority now is to figure out why someone wanted me out of the way," I said as I turned to leave. "Good night Chief, I'll see you in the morning."

Sully raised his hand and waved. "Alright, you know how to reach me if you need anything."

I had wanted to talk with the Chief about this case anyway and had planned on taking him with me to the Cranes' cabin. Some things work out for the best; he was busy at the time and Chief Sully not being with me perhaps saved him, saved me or possibly saved both of us.

As I cautiously made my way to my quarters for the night, I thought to myself that Chief Sully had said more than he realized. It goes without saying; my senses were on high alert. Being shot at does that to a person. The Chief's initial thoughts were that the Crane case wasn't a murder/suicide. A gut with that many cop years and doughnuts behind it was a gut worth listening to.

It was getting late as I completed the short ride to my quarters. The cold air was good for clearing my thoughts and waking me up; just what I needed in order to get myself ready for a long night of reviewing this case file.

Chapter 4

Once I arrived at the Fish and Game shop and bunkhouse, I wasted no time getting the snowmachine inside the warm garage. The shop was normally empty about half the time as the Fish and Game crew that worked there lived in Fairbanks - this was a time it was empty. That meant the four man bunkhouse that was part of the shop was vacant, except for me. Pretty cozy accommodations with four bunks, a monitor stove for heat, an electric oven and cook top, microwave, table, chairs and cabinets. The drawback was that there was no running water. The honey bucket, or thunder mug as some people called it, was somewhat rustic and having to get jugs of water from BLM could be a pain in the neck, but what the heck, at least it was private. I would hate to stay there with three other people. That would be far too cozy.

I found some ramen noodles in a cabinet and believed they would make a good dinner. It's common to bring more food than you need and leave it, which makes it okay to use what is there if you get caught in a pinch and are unable to make a run to the local store. I was in no mood to stop off for anything. I didn't think I was in any danger right in town, but why take a chance?

While enjoying my meager meal, I thought about the events of the day. I had found out a few days before that I was tasked to come out and take a look at this case for a final time. I arrived to find that no one was told why I was here but it was clear that everyone knew I had come to town. Gossip seems to spread like wildfire in small towns. It was most likely common knowledge that I was on the way, even before I arrived. It's not common that a state investigator blows into town in rural Alaska. The Crane case was the only logical reason someone such as me would even be there right now.

Without telling anyone what I was doing, I jumped on a snowmachine and headed out to the Big Moose Lodge and checked out the caretaker's cabin. It was simple to figure out, I would guess. There was no other reason for my actions except to be looking into the Crane case. Someone became very worried as to what that was about. Could someone believe that there was something more to my trip other than just a routine review before closing the case for good? That has to be what happened: somebody became paranoid.

I decided that I needed to review this case file again. I also needed to call my supervisor. But first, I wanted to finish these awesome noodles.

I finished the light meal and then cleaned my dishes. I picked up my cell phone and dialed a familiar number.

It was only seven p.m. but it took several rings before someone picked up on the other end.

"Hello," the gruff voice of my supervisor, Mark Dillon, greeted me.

I furrowed my brow at the gruffness of Mark's hello. "Did I bother you Mark?" I replied.

Mark cleared his throat. "You're never a bother."

I paused briefly and then began. "I thought I would check in with you before it gets too late; I know you need your beauty sleep."

Mark chuckled; his voice seemed clearer now. It seemed as if I interrupted something. "I've slept half my life thinking it would make me look better; I've given up on that theory altogether. How was your day?"

I related everything that happened right up until I returned to the Fish and Game bunkhouse. I paused, but there was silence. "Did you go back to sleep?" I asked.

Mark cleared his throat a second time. "So, what you're telling me is that your check of the crime scene and review of the case file all fit the conclusion originally reached, that this was a murder/suicide, but as you're returning to town someone tries to punch your ticket. That doesn't make sense." Mark continued, "What are your thoughts about what happened? Do you think the Crane case is related to the attempt on your life?"

I sat back in my chair and stretched the legs of my six foot three inch frame out in front of me. "Mark, what I think is that I've stirred up a hornets nest. I've kicked the proverbial sleeping dog. There's something going on that is directly related to the Crane case and now it's my job to figure it out."

"Don't hold back," Mark said. "Give it to me straight."

"Always the comic," I quipped. "If it was you that had been shot at, you would be serious. How is Archie?"

"No worries, he's good." Mark assured me. "You know he'll be well cared for as long as you need."

"Thank you," I replied. "I'm going to go over this case file again. I'll call you tomorrow with any news."

Mark stifled a yawn. "Okay my friend, you be safe and I'll talk to you soon."

"You too Mark; go back to bed sleeping beauty," and with that, I hung up the phone. I grabbed the Crane case file and put it on the table in front of me. It was time to take a look at the facts with a new perspective.

I spent hours going over and over the report: interviews, case notes, photographs, lab reports and diagrams. Having seen the actual location of the deaths, much of this became even clearer and easier to understand. However, there seemed to be no evidence that this was anything other than a murder/suicide as first suspected.

The young couple came from Canada. There were no enemies known to them and nothing popped up in their past that would obviously lead to such a tragic end. Their consumption of alcohol seemed average and they had a good job. They were educated and had no history of drug usage. They seemed to be friendly enough according to those who knew them. Nothing from their past suggested that they had any criminal ties whatsoever. The couple had a few arguments but nothing violent or anything to suggest the husband would kill his wife and then himself. There had been no suicide note found, but it's well documented that more suicides occur without a note being left behind than those that do.

There had been no forced entry or sign of a burglary at the cabin. The couple had no money. They had a very small savings for a rainy day and that was about it and that was in a bank, not at their home. They owned nothing of any significant value. Their family had indicated that they both were content. All the lab tests and their wounds supported the current theory.

What were we missing? The owners of the lodge had been interviewed and they had no insight on what could have caused this tragic event. The only oddity that even made sense was that there was no more of a reason for this to be a murder/suicide than there was a reason for this to be a double murder.

Everyone believed it was *'cabin fever'* and left it at that particular explanation: an intangible conclusion that seemed to be a catch all for circumstances just like this one. Looking at the photos of Crane and his wife, it didn't seem logical that this man would turn into a monster for a brief instant and do the unthinkable.

After reviewing the stack of information over and over, I stretched out on my bunk and listened to music on my phone. I needed to relax and get some rest. It wasn't long before I drifted off to sleep. I dreamed of the cold, snow and ice.

I wasn't sure how long I had slept when I abruptly woke up. My heart was pounding. Did I hear a noise? I remained still and listened. Nothing! What made me wake up so suddenly? What time was it? A quick glance at the phone by my side revealed that it was only five-fifteen a.m. How long had I slept? I remained still and continued to listen. The slight click of the monitor heater and the whir of its fan broke the dead silence. It was a couple of hours earlier than I intended to wake up for the day, so I decided to just lie there with my eyes closed and continue to rest.

Sometime later, my eyes once again flew open. Photographs! I was looking at pictures of the victims, the crime scene itself. The photographs! I jumped out of my bunk and threw on the overhead light. The small LED clock by the stove read seven-ten a.m. I grabbed the case folder and pulled out the photos of both victims. Carefully, I looked them over, one by one. One photo in particular caught my eye. I looked closely at it and turned it around in my hands. Then I searched through the remaining photos and found others that captured the same object that had caught my eye. I scanned the scene diagram and then read some of the notes I had made and re-read some of the investigative notes in the original report.

How could we have all missed this? I had more questions and a new theory of what actually happened in that cabin last November. It was a murder alright, a double murder!

Chapter 5

I spent the next hour getting some breakfast together and washing up afterwards. Okay, pop tarts and tang may not qualify as the breakfast of champions but it was tasty enough. Or, at least it should have provided me with some energy from the sugar alone. I had called Chief Sully earlier and expected him to arrive to pick me up at any time. It seemed apparent to me that riding around in his Expedition was warmer, and hopefully safer if we were together.

I had some questions for Chief Sully and perhaps a visit with the trapper who had found the Cranes was in order. I wanted to see if my theory had any veracity or if I was just grasping at straws.

Within minutes I heard a vehicle pull up to the building. I was ready to go, so I opened the door and stepped outside. It was getting daylight and the temperature was no colder than about minus ten degrees Fahrenheit. Based on the weather forecast I had pulled up on my phone, it was supposed to be another clear and cold day. I waved at Chief Sully and he nodded. I secured the shop door and made my way around to the passenger side of the patrol vehicle, opened the door and slid onto the warm passenger seat. Who would have thought something to warm your car seat would be such a wonderful idea!

"Good morning Chief," I greeted Chief Sully. "I was hoping we could go to your office and go over a few things."

Chief Sully looked thoughtful and nodded. "Sure thing, I'm all yours. I want to get this thing solved. I don't like the idea of having someone in town who would take potshots at a cop. I could be next."

The Chief and I drove to his office in relative silence. It was clear that we both were deep in thought. The Chief was a good man; I could think of only a few men I would want helping me with this case. He was one of those men. This town was lucky to have him as their Chief of Police.

After arriving at the Chief's office, we went inside and closed the door behind us. Seated at his desk, Chief Sully picked up and dialed his phone. He told the person on the other end that he was busy until he informed them otherwise and unless it was a life or death emergency to take a message. I suspected he was speaking to Fanny.

Chief Sully hung up his phone and looked across his desk at me. "Okay, I'm all yours," he told me. "I've been thinking about this case since you left me last night. I can't think of anything else; this thing has me stumped."

I handed Chief Sully a few photos of the crime scene and asked him to look them over. He took the photos and studied them slowly, one at a time.

"Who was the first known person to see the Cranes after they were shot?" I asked.

Chief Sully put the photos on his desk. "Jerry Smart, a trapper friend of the couple."

"Okay, did he move or have any contact with any of the victims?"

"I spoke to Jerry at length. He never even made it inside the cabin," Sully said. "The door was locked but he was able to look inside and saw what he knew was a death scene; he came directly here. The fire chief and I were the first two who made it back to the scene and the cabin was locked tight. There was no way that Jerry could have even been inside, much less touch anything."

Referring to the report Chief Sully had prepared I continued. "In your report you wrote that you and the fire chief made entry into the cabin by forcing open the front door. You documented the condition of the door before and after your entry, which was good thinking. You then documented what you found inside with some photos, some of which I just showed you. I know that the fire chief, who is also a paramedic, verified that both victims were deceased before you secured the scene."

"Yeah," Chief Sully mused. "But I'm missing your point."

"Okay, Jerry Smart didn't touch the bodies; neither you nor the fire chief moved the bodies, did you? I mean, death was verified easy enough."

"Neither of us moved the bodies." Chief Sully's eyes lit up as though it had just occurred to him what I was talking about. "Absolutely, what you see in these photos is what we found. Jerry was never in there, and no one moved either body. We secured the scene and waited for investigators and crime scene techs from Fairbanks to arrive."

I watched the Chief as his mouth opened again but no words came out. He held up a photo and pointed to a small pool of blood on the floor at the front edge of the couch, at a point that was just under Jess Crane's right knee. A faint trail of blood about one quarter inch wide was on his pant leg directly above the blood on the floor under his knee. From the photos, the source of that blood could not be determined. More specifically, there was no logical explanation as to how that blood got there. The Chief had noticed the same suspicious blood stains that I had.

"Chief, what I believe happened is that someone shot Jess Crane and after a short amount of time repositioned his body to make it appear to be a self-inflicted gunshot wound. Jess was shot in the head in such a manner that he died instantly. There's no way he could have fallen forward enough to begin bleeding on his leg that way and then after a few minutes his body just flopped over onto its left side and carried the gun with it and then dropped it on the floor beneath its hand. In my opinion that scene was staged in order for it to look like a suicide."

It stands to reason that blood, just like water, will flow downhill and follow the path of least resistance. In the crime scene photos, Jess Crane was lying on that couch on his left side. His right hand was hanging over the front edge of the couch about midway up his chest and directly beneath his hand, on the floor, was the revolver that ballistic tests had verified as the weapon that was used to shoot both victims. The large caliber handgun had been traced back to Jess Crane.

With the exception of that questionable blood stain, there was plenty of blood and tissue exactly where you would expect it to be from that type of shooting event.

At first glance, the photos suggested that Crane was seated on the couch when he had been shot in the right temple. His body fell to the left which made perfect sense given that the force of the shot was from right to left. In short, it appeared that his body fell to the left and his hand flopped forward and the gun fell to the floor.

There was absolutely no chance for that questionable bloodstain to have been where it was unless he had slumped forward and blood began dripping onto his right knee and ran off onto the floor when Crane was first shot. Then his body was moved for some reason. I say that reason was to make his death look more like a suicide.

The lab reports revealed that gunshot residue was present on Crane's hands. He loved to target shoot by all accounts, so that wasn't surprising. But that blood evidence discrepancy was the first tangible evidence that supports my new theory. The Cranes were both shot in cold blood and it was carefully staged to look like a murder/suicide.

Before someone tried to take me out of the picture I would never have believed there was a problem with the current findings of the case. I was just a couple of hours away from returning to Anchorage and reporting to my supervisor that everything seemed just as it was originally reported and recommending to close the case as a murder/suicide.

Chief Sully sat back in his chair and removed his hat and rubbed his head with his right hand. "I don't know how I could have missed this. It's like one of those pictures you look at that are actually two separate images. When you finally see the second image, you can't believe that you didn't see it right off. This was right there staring me in the face."

"Don't blame yourself. Countless eyes viewed the actual scene and these photos, and for whatever reason this went unnoticed."

Now it was a brand new ballgame. I needed to get in touch with Mark Dillon and explain to him what I believed I had uncovered. An expert at blood flow and bloodstain interpretation had to examine these photos and get us their analysis. I needed to get back to the scene and take yet another look.

It looked as if the investigation had turned into a bona fide who done it. Six months after the fact, incredible!

Chief Sully excused himself and left the room to run an errand. I took the opportunity and called Mark back at his Anchorage office. Mark had been preparing to testify in a case he had helped the Sitka Police Department solve. It was a murder that occurred aboard a cruise ship that was docked at the small southeast town. Mark was a bit testy at first. Since his wife left him and took everything Mark had worked for, he had been testy so it came as no surprise.

"Hi Mark," I started the conversation. "I know you're busy but I believe I have a new direction on the Crane case."

I told Mark about my new theory. Mark had a copy of the case at his office and he was able to look at the photos of the crime scene and listen as I explained the blood flow issue and the discrepancy I found. Mark was a bit skeptical at first but as he looked long and hard at the photos I referred to he began to understand my theory.

"I have a friend who's an expert in bloodstain pattern analysis who works at a crime lab in Seattle," Mark said. "I think it would be a good idea for me to get his opinion on this before we get too far along just to find out there's another explanation we're not considering."

"Can you email him some digital photos and call in a favor for a quick response of at least a preliminary result?" I asked. "With the fact that someone took a shot at me, I would think the urgency to get this solved would have risen to a whole new level."

"Yeah, I'll get this going pronto," Mark said. "As soon as I get an answer I can let you know."

Before hanging up I thanked Mark once again for taking care of Archie. He told me to be careful and keep him posted.

Just about the time I finished my call to Mark, the door to the Chief's office opened. Chief Sully sauntered through the door and a young blonde haired man of about twenty-five years of age was on the Chief's heels.

Chief Sully stopped and faced me. "I'd like to introduce Kyle Jeffers. Kyle is one of my officers and has been on board for a bit over a year."

I stood and extended my right hand toward Kyle. "Jake Rohn. Very nice to meet you."

Kyle smiled as he shook my hand. "I've heard quite a lot about you from Chief Sully. I wanted to meet you in person."

I made a nodding gesture toward the Chief. "Well, I'll have to take a little bit of time and straighten out all the tall tales Chief Sully has spun about me."

Kyle grinned as he began turning back toward the door. "It was good meeting you. I'll let you two get back to your business."

Kyle stepped out of the office and closed the door behind him.

I sat back in my chair. "Seems like a good guy."

Sully eased back in his desk chair. "Yeah, he's doing pretty well. He just finished the academy classes in Fairbanks about a month ago. I've been seeing to his training myself, making sure that he meets all of the necessary requirements for police officers by the Alaska Police Standards Council." Sully picked up one of those stress squishy balls and began squeezing it, seemingly out of habit. "Kyle was raised on the east coast and spent a tour in the army as an infantry soldier. He did at least a year in Iraq. After he got out of the military he took a few jobs with a couple of different security firms across the country. He likes law enforcement and is drawn to the wide open spaces in Alaska. I swear he's always out on his skis or snowmachine during the winter or on his boat in the summer - camping, hiking or exploring. He's doing a good job for us but I figure he'll more than likely take what he has learned while working here and move on in a year or so."

When Sully paused I asked the obvious question. "What brought Kyle to Fort Yukon of all places?"

Sully hesitated before he answered that question; he took some time to think about his reply. "I hired Kyle in January of last year. He had actually visited Big Moose Lodge as a guest about four months earlier and spent some time exploring, like he always does. He called me a couple of weeks after he returned home. We had met briefly at the airport as he was leaving. He asked about applying if an opening came up since he liked the area so much. He filled out an application and the rest is history so to speak."

I wondered how many times in the last few minutes Sully had actually squeezed that ball. "If he does move on and lands a good cop job, you should be proud that you were responsible for training him well enough to make him a viable candidate."

Sully seemed to agree with what I said judging by his subtle nodding in the affirmative. After he had taken a moment to reflect on the hiring of Jeffers, it was back to the business at hand. "Okay, what do you think is our next step?"

He was right of course. We needed to make a game plan and get to figuring out what really happened in the Cranes' cabin last November. The sooner the better, in my opinion.

Chapter 6

I filled Sully in on my call to Mark. We both hoped that we could get some sort of official word fairly quickly about what the blood evidence seemed to be telling us.

We could have things all wrong. Perhaps someone stubbed their toe really bad and bled on the floor in that very spot before the shooting occurred.

It was almost ten a.m. "We should take a ride back up to the caretaker's cabin and look the scene over again. We can be back in a few hours, long before dark," I suggested.

Sully stood and grabbed his coat from a five foot tall coat rack near the door. "Okay, my machine is in the city shop. I can be ready to go in about twenty minutes."

Chief Sully and I left the office in his Expedition and he took me back to the Fish and Game building. I opened the door to exit the vehicle. "I'll be back to your office with my snowmachine in just a little bit."

I exited the police vehicle, closed the door and watched Sully drive away. Once inside, I donned my gear and checked out my snowmachine. I planned to take the same machine as I had the day before. That bullet hole would constantly remind me to keep my head up, and down, at the same time. Danger definitely lurks in unsuspecting places.

I performed a pre-ride check and used some stored gas to fuel up the snowmachine. When I was all set to go I pulled the recoil rope and started the machine and opened the overhead door and then drove out. It was another beautiful clear day, just as cold as the day before and every bit as stunning. I secured the shop and started out to meet Chief Sully.

We drove out of town in single file with me in the lead, following the same trail I had taken the day before. Chief Sully was decked out in arctic gear from head to toe. He had added a rifle in a scabbard attached to a rack on the back of his snowmachine. I thought that was a nice touch. He was riding the Cadillac of snowmachines compared to my basic Polaris trail machine with manual start and two-up seat. Sully was on a Polaris touring sled with wide skins on his front skis, electric start, heated seat, heated hand grips and a heated thumb throttle lever. There were gauntlets over the hand grips which pretty much kept your hands so warm that wearing heavy gloves wasn't necessary. I really liked how the back rest on his machine could be positioned more forward so that a single occupant had back support while riding. On a long ride, it was tiring not having lower back support - I could attest to that.

Additionally, the Chief's touring sled had a full dash of instruments which showed his speed, rpms, fuel levels and engine temperature. There was an aftermarket GPS mounted on the dash as well. I don't know what the high-tech suspension was on that machine though I was sure his ride was so smooth that he could carry a full glass of water at fifty miles per hour and not spill a drop. He didn't have a bullet hole located dead center of his windshield, though, I was doubtful if he wanted one.

We both were on high alert, aware of everything around us, as we made our way out of town, cautious of anything that would be suspicious. When we arrived at the location where I had determined the sniper had waited for me, I stopped and shut down my machine.

I pointed out details and explained to Sully what I had determined from the visible evidence the day before when I found that place. With a watchful eye looking out for anything potentially harmful, Chief Sully and I both scoured over the area hoping to find anything other than the imprints of tracks in the snow. We came up with nothing.

We continued down the trail and I stopped again when we reached the position where I had stopped my machine and my windshield had been murdered the day before. There was nothing there except the trail, snowmachine tracks and the impression my body made in the snow as I had hunkered down behind the only cover I had.

Sully looked around and walked a bit further down the trail, maybe ten paces. He stopped right where the tree line began. "What do you make of this?" He was pointing at a spruce tree next to the trail. About four feet from the base of the tree, there was a fresh hole visible in the tree trunk.

I moved forward and looked at Sully's find and could not help but notice that the hole seemed about the size of the tip of my pinkie finger. I looked back along the trail in the direction we had come from. It was obvious that the hole in the trunk of that tree would line up perfectly with a line drawn from where the sniper had taken their shot and the hole in the windshield of my snowmachine where it had been parked. I was confident that there was a rifle slug in the hole Sully found in the trunk of that tree.

Chief Sully dug into his crime scene kit and pulled out a set of needle nose pliers with plastic tips. These types of pliers made it possible to do things such as extracting bullets from trees without damaging or compromising them. After I took a few photos, Sully used a knife blade to widen the hole and then used the pliers to extract the suspected rifle slug that was embedded about two inches in the tree. I was right on the money. Chief Sully held up a perfectly mushroomed slug for us both to see. He then dropped the slug into a brown envelope he had also taken from his evidence kit. "Well, we have a bullet. All we need now is a gun to match it to. I'm no expert, but my money says that's a seven-millimeter slug, fairly common up here."

The sight of that rifle slug sent a cold shiver down my spine. Just like the feeling I had almost twenty hours earlier when I had luckily dodged it. Too close for comfort.

After we resumed our trek to Jess Crane's cabin, I settled down and concentrated my attention on the trail ahead and keeping us both safe. We didn't see a single person but, just as we crossed the Porcupine River, we did see a moose. We also saw a fox, several rabbits and dozens of ptarmigan. Within thirty minutes we were at the cabin, which was just as cold on the inside as it was on the outside.

There had been no heat in there since before the Cranes had died. In November, when the bodies had been discovered, the temperature was a mild ten degrees above zero. During the long winter, temperatures in the region had dipped to a bone chilling fifty degrees below zero at times.

The timeline of the Cranes' death could only be narrowed down to a seven day period between when they were last seen in town and the discovery of their bodies. History told us it was normal for the caretakers of the lodge not to be seen for weeks at a time once the lodge closed for the winter.

I stood looking at the couch where Jess Crane's body had been found. There was still some dried blood visible on the cover of the couch. Though the bodies and all evidence had been removed, the scene would remain sealed until released by the state attorney.

The location where Linda Crane had been found told a story of a brutal shooting and her body falling directly to the floor next to a wooden table. Blood spatter and stains made it obvious she had bled out where she fell and, judging from the wound to the back of her head, had almost certainly died before hitting the floor. It was believed she had died first. In reality, now I'm not so sure that was what actually happened.

I knelt next to the questionable blood stain on the floor in front of the couch. The two inch stain was still visible, but time and maybe some small rodents had all but obliterated it. I was able to scrape up enough of the blood residue that, hopefully, it could be tested at the lab in Anchorage.

Chief Sully was conspicuously silent as I looked things over for a third and fourth time. Even with the extra scrutiny of the scene compared to the report and photos, there was nothing else that seemed out of place other than that two inch blood stain in front of the couch. Either that blood belonged to someone other than Jess Crane or it was Jess Crane's blood, which meant someone moved his body after he died. That would positively rule out murder/suicide. For the body of Jess Crane to be moved, someone else must have been there.

I walked over and stood next to Chief Sully. "Well, what do you think?"

Sully exhaled a long breath. "Standing here and looking at all of this again, I think a lot of things. I think these people were brutally murdered. I think I would like five minutes alone with the person who would do such a horrific thing."

I put my hand on the Chief's shoulder. "We're going to figure this thing out."

We were a somber pair as we prepared to leave the cabin. Having to relive the horrible event that occurred there was a tough thing to do, but we had to get through the ordeal in order to solve the case. The Cranes' deserved to have the truth be known as to what happened to them. If Jess Crane wasn't responsible, it was our job to find out who was.

"Let's take a look around the lodge since we're so close," Sully suggested.

"Okay, that seems like a good idea. We have plenty of time before it gets dark."

I followed as the Chief started out on his machine in the direction of the lodge. Within days of the Crane couple's death, new caretakers had been hired to watch over the lodge for the winter. The owners decided to hire a local couple who lived in Fort Yukon - Twila and Buster Sharp. They were lifelong residents of the area and hard workers by all reports.

As we drove around the huge lodge building and all the cabins and outbuildings, about fifteen in all, it was clear that Twila and Buster were doing an excellent job. Heavy snow load had been removed from the roofs. The trails between buildings were cleared and open. All the doors and windows were secured with shutters and crossbars. That was more to keep bears out of the buildings than to keep people out. A bear rummaging through the building looking for food that he was able to smell was capable of creating more damage than you could possibly imagine.

Our check around the lodge didn't produce any burning questions, or answers for that matter. Chief Sully had seen that setup for the last few years and he didn't note anything that seemed out of the ordinary.

I led our return trip to Fort Yukon. We saw a pair of majestic moose in a clearing about two miles from the lodge. These animals were massive and simply fantastic to watch. About seventy-five yards away, both animals merely watched us pass. The larger of the two animals stomped one of its front hoofs and swung its massive head back and forth. The moose was making it clear we were on its turf and we best steer clear. We did just that.

Upon arriving in town, we stopped our machines in front of the PD. I removed my hood and face gator. "It's already four-twenty; we were out a little longer than I thought we would be."

Sully pulled back his hood and uncovered his face too. "How about I buy you dinner tonight? You look as if you could use a hot meal . . . unless you prefer to eat spam and pilot bread."

"Yes, on the dinner," I suppressed a frown. "Not just no, but hell no to the spam!"

The Chief laughed. "How long do you need? I'll pick you up at your bunkhouse."

"How about in an hour?" I inquired, hoping the Chief would go for that.

"I'll be there at about five-thirty. I need to do a few things at home after I check in with Fanny. Claire has a school board meeting and I have to fend for myself anyway."

Chief Sully hopped off his machine and went inside.

Chapter 7

I made the one minute ride to the Fish and Game building without misfortune and put the machine I had been driving away. I was eager to get inside and place a call to Mark, hoping to find out if his source was able to make any progress analyzing the photos of the crime scene. Once inside the bunkhouse, I retrieved my cell phone and turned it on. With no service available away from town I had left the phone behind to charge. After the damn thing finished its startup routine, it chimed and buzzed twice, indicating I had two messages.

The first voicemail was from Mark. He sounded winded. Maybe it was his excitement that I was hearing.

"Jake, my source has given me a preliminary report on his analysis of the bloodstain evidence in question. He said that from his initial viewings of the photos it appears quite clear to him that the body of Jess Crane was moved within probably a two minute period after being shot. He reached this conclusion due to changes in the patterns of blood flow on the victim and inconsistencies with some blood pooling noted in the photos. It's a long story but he'll

continue to examine the photos and then prepare a report of his findings. It's now official; this case is a double homicide. I'm making plans to travel there as quickly as I can. I'll be in touch."

I pushed the button for the second message. It was Whitney Cartwright.

"Jake, where have you been the last couple of days? I wanted to tell you that I had an awesome time last Friday. We have to do that again, hugs to you. Call me!"

Whitney. I haven't had any time to think about her the past few days. She was thirty-two years old, five foot eight inches tall, with long auburn hair, accentuated curves and a beautiful smile. I met her about six months ago. While preparing for a case at the courthouse in downtown Anchorage, I drew the short straw and had to make the coffee run. I didn't even like coffee.

With money and six complicated coffee orders in hand, I exited the court building and walked over to the Cup-A-Joe coffee cart that was located in the center of the square adjacent to the courthouse and was surrounded by various other buildings and offices. Whitney was the young lady who helped me with that order. Her smile and tender nature struck me right in the heart. It had been more than five years since my engagement had ended in Colorado. I moved to Alaska not long afterward and, I'm ashamed to say, I haven't had any lasting relationship since I arrived. Sure, I'd actually seen a few women and stolen a couple of kisses but my heart was never in it. I stuck mostly to my work; I thought that was easier in the long run.

That was the case up until the time I laid eyes on Whitney. Being the astute investigator that I was, I could see she wasn't wearing an engagement or wedding ring. I generally felt a level of confidence around women who appealed to me, but with Whitney I felt like an absolute moron with his mouth taped shut and his hands tied behind his back.

For the remainder of that day I couldn't get my mind off of that woman. By the end of the week I had made at least six trips to Whitney's cart. I engaged her in small talk and gathered as much information about her as I could, such as she was single, she was from Anchorage and was attending the University of Alaska at night in order to obtain a degree in business and that she owned and was the sole employee of the Cup-A-Joe.

Another thing I discovered was that I hated coffee more than I ever knew. The best thing that I learned after about two weeks of visiting

Whitney on a daily basis was that she was willing to accompany me to dinner sometime.

Since then, there had been a lot of *'sometimes.'* Whitney stirred something inside of me that was dormant for a long time. We had been seeing one another rather steadily now for months and the best part of our relationship was that she didn't pressure me. She was content that we kept our own places; no need to rush. I think the only belongings we had at each other's homes was a toothbrush. The relationship was moving along at just the right pace. Maybe I should let her know I've been busy and would be home in a few days.

I must have been daydreaming about Whitney for quite a while. An incessant honking from a vehicle outside brought me out of my reverie. I grabbed my coat and headed to the door. Chief Sully was waiting in his Expedition. I hopped in and we drove over to the local eatery.

A soon as we were seated, I filled Sully in on the message from Mark. The Chief was happy that Mark was on his way to help. His elation that the case was officially a double murder was a bit more subdued. I had the impression that Chief Sully felt bad that the entire matter had been misinterpreted for so many months. He didn't follow his gut on this one. I couldn't think of a thing to say that would help him feel better. If, in fact, this turns out the way it's heading, he can't blame himself. So many made exactly the same oversight.

We ate pretty much in silence. A few customers were seated near us and we didn't want to make our progress front page news so to speak. We were tired and the food was excellent. Actually, we both were stumped on how to proceed with the investigation anyway. I guess we would go back to the beginning and start all over again and make sure other subtle clues weren't missed. It's similar to when you write a report and after you check it over a dozen times to make sure there are no errors, someone else picks it up and immediately points out a mistake in the first paragraph. Your mind has compensated for that error and you just can't see it, no matter how many times you look it over.

Just as we were finishing our meal, a grey haired sixty-something gentleman approached us and pulled out a chair and sat down. He looked squarely at me and offered me his right hand and introduced himself. "Merle Davis."

I shook his hand. "Jake Rohn."

Merle turned toward Sully. Talk about cutting to the chase and getting directly to the point. I liked Merle.

"Chief, sorry to bother your dinner but I have a complaint. Yesterday about four in the afternoon I was walking back home from the post office. You know I walk up to the post office almost every day at that time and get my mail and then walk home. You've seen me a couple hundred times."

Sully nodded. "You're right Merle, nearly every day. I see you sometimes."

Merle continued. "Well, yesterday that damn Albert Shelton practically ran over me on his snogo. If it wasn't for my intuition and cat-like reflexes I would be dead right now. I heard him coming and jumped to the side of the road. Albert must have been doing eighty miles an hour as he flew by me on that rocket sled of his. Albert always drives like a crazy maniac. He was coming from the direction of that trail leading out of town toward the Porcupine River and he had that big hunting rifle of his slung across his back. I know that loser was out poaching moose. I could understand if he had a twenty-two rifle for hunting rabbits, but not a seven-millimeter rifle! Does he think we're all stupid? You need to do something about that clown before he hurts somebody."

Chief Sully and I looked at one another; we knew exactly what our next move was. I was correct with my earlier impression; I liked Merle a great deal!

Chapter 8

My second night in Fort Yukon was long and restless. I was tired but didn't sleep well at all. I had that damn nightmare again. I pretty much spent the night tossing and turning afterwards. I stayed in bed as long as I could stand just lying there. I eventually decided to get up and get moving. It was just a little after six a.m.

I checked my phone and found that I had a text message from Mark. Bad news! Mark had landed in Fairbanks and while he was waiting for a flight to Fort Yukon he was notified of an officer involved shooting in Delta Junction, a small community about one-hundred miles south of Fairbanks. He was diverted there. He wished me the best and told me to keep my head down and *'watch my top knot.'* That was Mark's favorite saying.

I wasn't sure when he might receive it, but I answered Mark's text and told him we might have caught a break and that I'd keep him informed. I also asked him what he had done with Archie since he had left Anchorage.

Whitney, I needed to let her know something. After leaving her home on Saturday morning, I hadn't been in contact with her at all. It wasn't unusual for us to go several days in a row without hearing from one another. Her school and business, coupled with my job and travels, took up quite a large amount of time and kept us apart. She was a special lady, there was no denying that. She was understanding, smart, and beautiful.

I didn't want Whitney to become overly worried, so I fashioned a brief text message and sent it to her.

"Hi, working on a case up north that has taken some unexpected turns. Not sure when I will return to Anchorage – miss you!"

I found myself something to eat, then straightened up and sat back in my chair and turned my thoughts to all the events that had transpired the past two days. In police work, I had learned to be prepared for anything. I could never have dreamed of these circumstances, especially an attempt on my life.

Merle Davis was an absolute godsend. Unknowingly, he handed us perhaps a case breaking clue. Albert Shelton was put right at the top of the list of suspects who might have shot at me. Actually, at the moment Albert

Shelton was the only suspect on that list. A witness had seen him speeding away from the area where someone had taken a shot at me. It was the right time of day and he had a rifle with him that could possibly be matched to the bullet we had extracted from the tree trunk. That sounded good enough for me. I'd like to get my hands on that rifle for a ballistics test!

I warmed up some water and waited for Sully to arrive. It was ten minutes after eight when I heard a loud knock on the door.

"Come on in Chief."

Sully came through the door holding up a folder. "Here's the information you asked for. I could've told you everything you needed to know about Albert Shelton. He's been a thorn in this town's side for more than half his life!"

I was up and looking for two cups and some instant coffee. "Good morning Sully."

Sully took a chair at the table. "Oh, good morning. How'd you sleep?"

I brought the makings for coffee to the table. "Sleep! What's that exactly?"

Sully began making a cup of instant coffee. "Why two cups? Have you changed your habits? I didn't think you cared for the stuff."

As I stirred my own cup of coffee I knew I wouldn't drink a drop of it. "It's a long story Chief. So tell me all about Albert Shelton."

Chief Sully opened the folder. "Albert is thirty-six and has lived locally for at least twenty years. His family is from a village about fifty miles north of here. Albert didn't finish school."

I continued to stir my coffee, lifted it to my lips and blew on it but I never so much as took a sip.

Sully looked at me as though I had lost my mind. "He has had about thirty arrests and half as many convictions, all misdemeanors such as theft, assault, bootlegging and weapons offenses. He had a couple of felony charges but they were all either dropped or reduced down to misdemeanors."

I continued to stir, lift, blow and then set the cup back in front of me. What I didn't want to tell Chief Sully was one of those thoughts that one man would never tell another. Having the coffee in hand, but not drinking any and just nursing it like I was made me feel close to Whitney.

"So, what does Mr. Shelton do for fun when he's not defending himself in court?"

"You name it," Sully answered. "He traps, does some odd labor jobs and has been known to fight fires with BLM during the summer months. Personally, I think he does some small time selling of drugs and alcohol bootlegging but I don't have any real proof."

I retrieved a paper towel to wipe up some coffee that had splashed out of my cup and onto the table. "Do you have any idea of a connection between Albert and the Cranes or the lodge?"

Chief Sully began making himself a second cup of instant coffee. "Nothing specific that I'm aware of, but it's possible that anyone from town could be out that way at one time or another. I have no information that he even knew the Cranes."

I'm not sure what came over me but I braved it and actually tasted my coffee. The stuff needed a lot more sugar and cream in my opinion. I just don't know how people actually drink so much coffee and seemingly can't function without it.

"We're kind of making a big assumption. Even if it was Albert who shot at me we're assuming that it had something to do with this case. Maybe he had been hunting out of season like Merle suggested and thought I saw something and was trying to scare me."

Sully shook his head. "So, you like a little coffee with your cream and sugar?"

"There you go again Chief; you're a funny man, but it still tastes awful and I'm not even sure why I tried it in the first place!."

"To each his own, as they say," replied Sully. "It all seems too coincidental; Albert has to be involved somehow. I just can't believe that he would have randomly shot at you. Why would he chance such a thing without a very good reason?"

Chief Sully made complete sense, more sense than I was making with my coffee. "So how do you figure we should handle this then? I mean, you know the guy and have dealt with him before."

"If you're asking me, I think I should confront him regarding a complaint of him driving reckless; after all, I did get a complaint." Chief Sully stated in a matter-of-fact manner. "That's legit and we can see how he reacts when he sees you."

I contemplated trying the coffee again but thought better of it. "That's a good idea; we can go in your rig. Since it has clouded up some it's not as cold, but it would be better than snowmachines if you ask me."

The Chief drained his cup, "Let's roll."

With that, we exited the bunkhouse and got into the Expedition. During our brief drive we discussed our approach to Albert's place. He lived alone on the edge of town in a two room wood framed house. We decided the best thing for us to do was to park out of sight and carefully approach the house. Then we would step up on the porch and stand to one side of the front door and knock. That was exactly what we did.

A male voice, which I assumed to come from Albert Shelton, shouted out from inside the home. "Who is it?"

I looked at Sully and whispered. "Is that Albert?"

Sully nodded in the affirmative and answered the voice from inside the small home. "Chief Sullivan, Albert, I need to speak with you."

Again, I heard Albert's voice from within the home. "Give me a minute and I'll be right out," and then we heard some rustling sounds from inside the house.

Seconds later we heard a loud noise from the back of the small home and a male figure ran around the side of the house, to a snowmachine parked close by. He jumped onto the machine and fired up the engine. The figure, who I now assumed to be Albert, sped off down the road toward the airport.

I heard Chief Sully yell. "Albert! Wait! I just want to talk!"

It was too late. Albert Shelton had zoomed down the road on his snowmachine as though his ass was on fire and his head was catching. Even if he could have heard the Chief, I doubt whether he would have listened anyway.

There were no paved roads in town. The snow and hard ice packed on top of the dirt and gravel roads served as a perfect track for the speeding snowmachine.

Chief Sully and I scrambled off the porch and to his vehicle to give chase. The snowmachine was far too fast for our vehicle and had at least a hundred yard head start by then. We saw Albert turn to the left when he reached the airport and then he proceeded directly toward the Yukon River. We followed as best we could.

We watched the machine and rider as they sped down the barge landing ramp and onto the frozen Yukon River. Shelton apparently intended to reach the other side of the river which was a half mile away. We were forced to stop at the barge landing as there was no way we could follow him onto the river in our vehicle.

As the snowmachine was about a quarter mile away, we saw the rider turn to look back towards us. As the rider turned to look forward again, we saw the brake light illuminate on the snowmachine. Then, as if by magic, both the machine and rider simply disappeared from sight.

I was stunned for a moment. I couldn't believe what I had just witnessed. Where did Albert go so suddenly? It was a wide open space. How could he have gotten away so quickly?

"Holy shit!" exclaimed Chief Sully. He keyed the mic on his police radio. "Fanny! I'm at the barge landing. Have the fire chief get a crew on snowmachines here right away; Albert Shelton has gone through the ice on the river about halfway across. We need help here now!"

Chapter 9

Only a few minutes had passed when the fire chief, Greg Sharp, showed up on a snowmachine. Within thirty seconds two more men on machines arrived. They had ropes and grappling hooks as part of the gear they had brought with them. I found out later that Greg was the twin brother of the new caretaker of the Big Moose Lodge.

Chief Sully had briefed Greg by the time the other two riders arrived on scene. The three of them drove out onto the ice, following the tracks of Shelton's machine. About halfway across we saw the men stop and dismount their machines. It seemed that they were peering down into a hole in the ice at that location. We watched as they put the ropes and hooks down into the hole in the ice, apparently in hopes of locating Albert under the water.

Chief Sully explained that it would be best if we stayed out of the way of these men. They could write a book on search and rescue efforts in water and under the ice. Sully continued and explained that a few times a year a resident either falls into water from a boat or through an opening in the ice and the results were usually not positive.

The location where Albert had apparently driven into open water on the river was notorious for surprising riders. Despite the fact that open water often appears in that very location every winter, probably due to some kind of current or underwater spring, it has taken numerous lives over the years.

We watched as a few more people joined in on the search for Albert and his machine. After about thirty minutes, Greg returned to where Chief Sully and I waited at the barge landing.

"Chief," began Greg, "The fresh tracks of a snowmachine go down onto the river and lead right to that open hole in the ice. I know the river is about twenty feet deep at that spot and the open lead is about ten feet wide and thirty feet long. The river ice itself is two feet thick. That spot opens up about every winter."

Chief Sully grimaced. "What do you think Greg?"

Greg let out a sigh. "I've seen this too many times. There's no open water downstream. If Albert didn't come out of the same hole he went in then that means he's under the ice. Chief, now we're looking for a body."

"Damn!" I quietly exclaimed.

Chief Sully was quick to provide direction. "Okay Greg, you guys get together what you need to begin a search. I know you have the numbers of all the search members. I'll set up an account at the store for supplies and with the fuel company so that you guys have what you require to continue searching. Keep me posted on your progress."

Greg got back on his machine. "Sure thing Chief, we'll keep you informed."

Greg started his snowmachine and headed back out onto the frozen river.

Chief Sully and I made the quick trip back to his office where he immediately picked up his office phone and called the managers at the local store and the fuel company in order to open a charge account. Another call was made to the statewide search and rescue coordinator. After briefing him, Sully answered a few questions, made a few notes and then hung up the phone. Then he briefed Kyle Jeffers on what had occurred so that Kyle could provide information to next of kin or friends of Albert as they would hear about what happened and start calling in. After his meeting with Kyle, the Chief walked over to the city manager's office and let him know what had taken place. He then returned to his office and slumped down in his chair.

Sully planted his forehead into his left hand and rubbed his temples with his thumb and fingers. "What the hell is going on here? I've spoken to Albert so many times that I can't even remember how often it has been. I've even arrested him on a few occasions and I've never had any trouble with him. Albert bolting like that just makes me even more convinced he was somehow involved in this mess and is the one who shot at you."

I agreed with the Chief. "You know we need to prove that one way or another and Albert was our only lead. I don't mean to sound inconsiderate but our only lead is apparently now at the bottom of the Yukon River. I think that we should prepare a search warrant for Albert's home based upon all the information we have. Getting our hands on his rifle alone could help answer many of our questions. Who knows what else we could find in his house that might shed some light on this entire case?"

We got busy and drafted probable cause for a search warrant which would allow us to search the home of Albert Shelton. Mainly, we would be looking for any rifles, ammo, cell phones and connections to the Cranes. We spent about two hours and when finished, believed we had put together a solid document. I called Anchorage and spoke to a prosecutor. I asked him to review what we had drafted and hopefully approve it so that we could take it before the local magistrate.

After faxing copies of the search warrant back and forth with some corrections and additions, we had a final copy approved by the prosecutor's office in-hand. In the meantime, Chief Sully had called in Officer Dale Mason to secure the residence of Albert Shelton. Officer Mason was to remain at the residence and make sure no one entered it and especially that nothing was removed.

I had a calm confidence in Dale Mason. He was still young and rather inexperienced but he had a way of relating to people on so many different levels that I knew he would make a good cop. He resembled movie star Tom Selleck.

Chief Sully and I tracked down the magistrate who was taking his lunch break at his own office. He was brown bagging it. Magistrate Preston was a short, balding and rather plump man who looked to be about sixty years old. His desk was filled with papers and books to the point I couldn't understand how he was able to find or keep up with any work he was trying to accomplish there. A huge ashtray sat on the corner of his desk and was completely full of cigarette butts.

"Magistrate Preston, this is Investigator Jacob Rohn from the States Attorney General's office." Chief Sully continued the introduction. "Rohn is here looking into the Crane case which we now believe to be a double homicide based on newly acquired evidence. We've brought a search warrant for you to look over and hopefully approve. Our goal is to search the residence of Albert Shelton since at this moment he appears to be a person of interest in the case."

Magistrate Preston looked over the top of his glasses at Sully and then back at me, and then stuck out his right hand. "Nice to finally meet you Mr. Rohn. I've heard of you and have looked forward to the opportunity to meet you. Word is you've been here a couple of days looking into this case." He took the documents from me. "It seems there are no secrets around here. I'm not surprised you think this may be a double homicide. I never really believed young Mr. Crane could kill anyone."

The magistrate silently read over our search warrant documents. He often shook his head up and down while reading. When he was done, he removed his reading glasses and looked directly at me. "Has this been approved by a prosecutor?"

"Yes sir," I said to the magistrate. "This is a fax copy but those are his initials at the bottom."

Magistrate Preston replaced his glasses and after I swore to the truth of the documents, I signed them. The magistrate applied his signature which authorized the legal search of the Albert Shelton residence. We received the appropriate copies and the warrant was properly logged into the court database.

"Good hunting gentlemen," added the magistrate as he showed us out of his office.

We thanked him for his time and we drove over to Albert Shelton's home. Dale Mason was parked in front of the home just as instructed. Chief Sully and I got out and approached Mason.

Mason waited until we are at his vehicle before he rolled down the driver's door window and addressed us. "All secure Chief, no one in or out."

"Very good," replied the Chief. "Now get your evidence kit and come inside and help."

Inside, we searched the small residence from top to bottom. All that we found and took as evidence was a seven-millimeter magnum bolt action rifle that was in a corner near the front door, one box of seven-millimeter rifle ammo and a cell phone that was charging on the counter. We weren't able to find another item in the house that suggested any connection with the Cranes or Big Moose Lodge. The rifle was of interest, of course, and cell phones were on the warrant since phone records could help out by showing who Shelton had been talking to. We did find a notepad on the table with the number *'three-o-three five-five-five eight-four-four-eight'* and the name *'Marcus'* written on it. Nothing else seemed even remotely significant.

Once completed with our search and securing the residence, we returned to the Chief's office with our evidence.

Chapter 10

Later that afternoon, Chief Sully checked in with Greg Sharp. After several hours of searching for Albert Shelton without success, the team planned to stop when visibility deteriorated to the point their safety became an issue as the sun lowered in the sky. Conditions were dangerous enough as they worked around a huge hole in the ice but as it became darker, that level of danger increased. The search team would continue their efforts the following morning.

We called the State Crime Lab in Anchorage and spoke with one of the firearms examiners that just happened to be available; we were fortunate he worked late. We asked for some advice on how to handle our firearm evidence, specifically the rifle and the recovered slug from the tree. We wanted to know if it was possible to get the slug that had been recovered from the tree trunk compared to a control slug fired from the rifle recovered from Shelton's home, at least we would know if we were on the right track.

Since timing was crucial, he suggested that we take 'one to one' photos of the bullet we had found in the tree and a control bullet fired from the seven-millimeter rifle recovered from Shelton's house. The idea was to take several photos each of the evidence slug and the control slug. An examination of the photos by the expert would likely provide initial findings accurate enough to determine if both slugs were indeed fired from the same weapon.

It was painstaking but there was a huge water trough in the city shop that we fired a round into from the seven-millimeter rifle we seized. We retrieved the fired bullet and Chief Sully enlisted the aid of Kyle Jeffers in taking some digital photos of the two slugs. Kyle was a budding photographer and had digital photography equipment advanced enough to take the photos of the two slugs as described by the expert. Once completed, we emailed the pictures to the firearms examiner in Anchorage.

If we had done a suitable job photographing the evidence, we would get some preliminary findings about the slugs based on a comparison of the photos fairly quick. Comparing the photos wouldn't be one-hundred percent accurate, but it certainly would give us enough information until an actual physical evaluation could be made. With the distance and time it took to travel to Anchorage from Fort Yukon, it would be a few days before the evidence could be received at the lab and then processed in person.

"Well Chief, it's a good thing that you have Kyle on board," I said. "I wouldn't know what a macro lens was if it fell from the sky and hit me on the head."

Nodding in agreement Chief Sully replied. "The two slugs at least seemed to be the same size. If the slug we found in the tree is a seven-millimeter; that's half the battle."

We both sat in silence for a moment. I dug my phone from out of my pocket and dialed Mark Dillon's number. Once again all I reached was his voicemail. For the third time I left a message and asked Mark to call me.

I used Chief Sully's office computer to check my email. As anticipated, I had an email from Mark's blood pattern analysis expert in my inbox. It had been sent to Mark and me.

I printed off the two page document and read it aloud to Chief Sully. The report contained a good bit of data about blood flow related to the method of injury, gravity, etc., but the final paragraph told it all.

"Based on the discernible change of direction of blood flow on both arms of the victim and an unexplained pooling pattern of blood to the victim's front, it's the conclusion of this examiner that the victim's upper body had been moved to his left approximately twelve to twenty four inches, within

approximately two minutes or less after the victim had been shot in the right temple."

What that meant to me was that a dead body couldn't rearrange itself unless acted upon by an outside force. In the particular situation at hand, that outside force had to be the person who shot and killed Jess Crane or at least a person who was present when someone else shot and killed Jess Crane. I can see this happening many different ways but at the very least there was somebody in the Cranes' home who shot and killed both of them and before leaving they adjusted the body of Jess Crane and left the handgun in a position to give the scene the appearance of a suicide.

I handed the report to the Chief. "Now I think we have even more questions."

Chief Sully finished scanning the report. "Okay, even if we seem to have proof that this could have more than likely been a double murder, the biggest two questions are who is responsible and why?"

"Start at the beginning."

"What?" asked the Chief.

"Start at the beginning; we were going to start at the beginning of the investigation and evaluate everything to ensure there wasn't other things that were missed," I said. "We've been doing so many other things that we have yet to go back to the beginning."

Sully finally caught on. "Alright, we've been to the scene, and looked over the reports and photos. Most of the evidence is in Anchorage."

"That's just it Chief. Most, but not all, of the evidence is in Anchorage."

I referred to a page of the report listing items originally removed from the cabin when the crime scene was first examined. "There are some papers, books, photos, a journal and personal belongings that weren't sent to the lab. According to the report these things were kept here."

"You're right! I'd almost forgotten about those. There are four boxes of what was considered non-essential evidence that has been kept right here in our evidence locker," said Chief Sully, suddenly remembering. "We intended on releasing all of it to their next of kin once the case was concluded and we had the go ahead from the state attorney to do so. I'll get those boxes and we can go through each of them and perhaps we'll find something that we missed or perhaps see something that looks different now."

I assisted Chief Sully in retrieving the four cardboard boxes that were stored in an evidence room. Each was about the size of a banker's box you would use to keep office files stored away.

"Well Chief, I'll take two and you can have two. It's getting late, so I'll take mine back to the bunkhouse and spend the evening going through the contents. Hopefully, one of us will find something that will help."

Chapter 11

After spending some time visiting with Kyle and Dale, Chief Sully dropped me off at the bunkhouse. I lugged in the two boxes of evidence. My evening's work.

I checked my phone hoping to have a message from Mark but there was none. Having worked on a few similar cases, I knew that officer involved shootings could turn into a tremendously difficult task. I didn't have any information on what had occurred but I knew that Mark and those there to help him were good at what they did. They'll get that situation under control. I had enough going on to keep me occupied.

I did have a message from Whitney. She understood that I was busy and wanted me to be careful. How understanding can one woman possibly be? I felt guilty that even though I felt so drawn to her, that I knew I loved her, I had never told her so. I wondered when my heart would be ready for love again. It had been more than five years since my engagement ended. I sat there and daydreamed of my last night with Whitney. That had been almost a week now. She was so pleasing and passionate. I often wondered how she truly felt about me. That was one of my hang ups. She hadn't ever really said how she felt about me. I guess I have just allowed myself to believe that she loved me. It was as if she was the same as me in the sense that she didn't have to say things out loud in order for them to be true.

Maybe I'm the foolish one, allowing someone to get that close to me once again. You would think I had learned my lesson. It would be a good thing to know how she really did feel about me. Then again, maybe I didn't really want to know.

Enough of that nonsense. I needed to get busy with the work at hand. I had two boxes of evidence to sift through in hopes of finding something to help this investigation.

Most of what I found in the boxes consisted of personal belongings of the Cranes. There was a small amount of jewelry - mostly costume stuff that would have no real worth except for maybe sentimental value. A man's watch and two wedding bands rounded out the jewelry. There were some small clothes items such as hats and gloves - nothing that added up to any useful clues. I found a folder filled with different types of receipts. I guessed that was for taxes based on the types of receipts it contained. A checkbook and an envelope with about one-hundred dollars cash inside it was in one of the boxes.

At the bottom of one box was a hand written journal and an old map of the region. The journal seemed to have been authored by Jess Crane, judging by the way the entries were written. It didn't have an entry for each day, but at least three or four per week. The journal contained basic everyday events the couple did or things they saw from the time they arrived in Alaska. There were many entries pertaining to their work to begin with, and then as time went by the entries were reduced to things such as camping trips and the fishing they had done, to include some drawings of favorite camping or fishing sites and areas they had explored. They both were learning to enjoy the wilderness and exploring Alaska. The couple had come from a more populated area in Canada and such wilderness was all new to them.

I finished the journal and that concluded my search of those two boxes of evidence. Nothing had jumped out at me as being important. I made myself some dinner, ate and then cleaned up. It was almost ten o'clock, so I decided to call Chief Sully and find out how things turned out with his two boxes of evidence.

"Evening Chief, how's it going with you?"

"Not so bad, the wife and I just finished a late supper."

Knowing what the answer would likely be, I had to ask. "What did you find in those boxes of evidence?"

"I went through both boxes piece by piece," said the Chief. "I didn't find anything of interest. I found some banking documents, a couple of books, and a few small items of clothing, hunting knives, photos and what I believe were letters from home."

"No signed confession or big red arrow pointing at a clue?" I asked.

"I went through it all. It does re-affirm what we already knew. The Cranes were certainly an average couple."

"You know what Chief? That's all I seem to have found as well. Tomorrow let's see if we can get into that cell phone we seized at Shelton's. Perhaps we can find a phone number or something that can really help us out. We can certainly use a break in this case; something that would bust this thing wide open would be just the ticket."

"Something will turn up; we just have to keep pushing forward. You can never tell when or what will cause a puzzling investigation to all of a sudden come together. I've been at this sort of thing for longer than I can remember. Good things come to those who are constantly working hard. Some people will tell you that since we're in such a small town everything is so much easier, but nothing could be farther from the truth. There are a lot of dynamics going on here that make it even more difficult if you ask me."

How about that! Chief Sully was giving me a pep talk now. Before, he was the doubtful one. Now that I'm the one who is so unsure, the Chief was quick to provide encouragement. The more I worked with that man the more I appreciated what he knew and how he handled himself.

"Thanks Chief, I'm really emotionally involved now and want to get this figured out. You and I are the only people who can speak for Jess and Linda Crane at this point. We can't bring them back but we can put a monster away and provide closure to their families and hopefully ease their suffering."

We said our pleasantries and then hung up. This entire business was driving me crazy. The more we looked, the less we knew.

Another long day would most certainly turn into another long night.

Chapter 12

The following morning I decided to take an early spin around the town on my snowmachine, just to see what was happening.

I toured all the trails and roads. Not much to see that early in the day on a cold spring morning in Fort Yukon, Alaska. It was beginning to get daylight out and a few people were stirring about. All I really accomplished was to get cold. I wound up at the police department building and went inside. The cold air had numbed my face and hands.

"Good morning Fanny," I said as I entered the office while rubbing my hands together hoping to get the feeling back in them.

Fanny looked up. "Good day to you. How are things going?"

"Well," I scratched my head not really sure what to say. "It could be colder; I suppose things are going good."

I wasn't sure how much Fanny knew about how all the recent events fit together, so I decided to change the subject. "Is the Chief in his office?"

Fanny nodded to one side, making an indication down the hall. "Yeah, he came in a while ago and I think he's in his office."

I thanked Fanny and headed down the hall. The Chief's office door was closed, so I knocked and waited for a response.

"Come on in," I heard the voice of Chief Sully from the other side of the door.

I opened the door and took a seat in the empty chair in front of the Chief's desk.

Chief Sully was reading over some papers. He put down the papers and looked over at me. "I spoke to Greg Sharp a little while ago. The search team will be resuming their systematic hunt for Albert Shelton this morning. I also called the Search and Rescue Coordinator and filled him in on the progress of the search process."

I waited for the Chief to finish updating me before I asked him my burning question. "Any word on the bullet evidence we sent to the crime lab?"

The Chief nodded in the affirmative. "Yeah. In fact I was just reading an email when you knocked. The young man at the crime lab must have burned some midnight oil to get this done. At your request, the examiner sent his findings to us both. It seems that the slug we pulled from the tree trunk and the control slug fired from Shelton's gun are a match - they were fired from the same rifle. He will make a positive ID once he gets the actual evidence in hand. He also said that even though his findings are *'preliminary'*, there's no reason why we shouldn't continue our investigation knowing the two slugs are most certainly the same caliber and were fired by the same gun."

"That definitely helps us Chief, so now we know Shelton was gunning for me, and undoubtedly because of my trip up to the Big Moose Lodge and to the cabin where the Cranes were killed."

"That means Shelton is either responsible for the couple's death or at least is connected in some way," said Chief Sully.

"Now we have to figure out what that connection is."

Chief Sully stood, obviously in thought; he preferred to move about when he was thinking out loud. "You get here and you went straight to the cabin. On your way back Shelton ambushed you. We tried to contact Shelton and he was so hell bent on getting away from us that he drove into an open lead on the river and ended up dead himself. We searched his place and found the rifle, ammo and cell phone but nothing else that provided any explanation as to how he could be involved with the Cranes."

"I agree Chief, but we haven't looked at that cell phone. Who was Shelton talking to?"

Chief Sully sat back down. "I looked through the phone we took from Shelton's place. I made a list of all the incoming and outgoing calls for the last two weeks on that phone. Fanny is tracking those numbers down. With the exception of one number, they all were from Alaska." He reached for his phone and punched in the numbers to Fanny's extension, spoke to her and then hung up.

Within a few seconds Fanny entered the office. "Here you go Chief, a list of the numbers and the names they are listed to." She handed him a sheet of paper. "All of the numbers are local, except one. I could account for every number he called except the three-o-three area code number listed at the bottom. He received a call from that three-o-three number on the very day Jake came into town. He then called that same number much later the same day."

"Three-o-three area code," I said aloud. "The number we found on that pad at Albert's place was a three-o-three area code. That particular area code is Denver, Colorado. I recall that from the days I lived in Colorado Springs."

Sully looked up from the paper Fanny had given him. "Every number he called was to locals that I would never suspect to be capable of any wrong doing, much less of being part of some type of criminal conspiracy with Albert Shelton."

Fanny turned to leave the office. "You're welcome Chief, let me know if I can be of more help," she said as she exited and closed the door behind her.

Chief Sully and I both were so engrossed in thought that we didn't even notice Fanny or her touch of sarcasm as she stomped out of the office.

"Chief, the name with that three-o-three phone number written on that pad was *'Marcus'*, the same three-o-three number that was in the phone. I'll call a detective friend in Denver and see if I can pull some strings and find out about that number."

For the next hour I used one of the extra offices and called an old buddy who was a detective in Denver. After we chatted about old times and caught each other up on news for a bit, I gave him the phone number we had found in Shelton's phone and written down at Shelton's house. The detective assured me he could track the information down in a fairly short amount of time and would get back to me once he finished.

Chief Sully and I went to lunch and reviewed the details of this case, both old and new. We were no closer to an answer but decided it was time for us to talk to people in town who we knew had contact with the Cranes on almost a daily basis while they were here. We thought it was possible that someone may have spoken to the couple and acquired some helpful information but were completely unaware they possessed such crucial details.

It was reasonable to believe that even though the Cranes mostly kept to themselves, they had to go to the post office or stock up on supplies and buy fuel. They had plenty of contact with different people in town - even if it wasn't socially.

After lunch, we went back to the Chief's office. No sooner had we arrived than my cell phone rang. It was my detective friend from Denver.

"That was fast," I said to him.

"Did you expect any less from the best?" he asked.

"Ha ha, you got me there. What did you find out?"

He filled me in. "The number you gave me, three-o-three five-five-five eight-four-four-eight, is a prepaid cell phone number. Untraceable when bought with cash, which this one was. This phone had one dialed call and one received call to and from the same nine-o-seven area code number you gave to me when we first spoke. The phone hadn't been used before that or since and likely has been destroyed or otherwise put out of service because when we tried pinging it or calling it, we got zip. As for the name *'Marcus'*, I struck out there as well. That name has been used as a moniker for literally hundreds of losers in our computer database. I asked around if anyone had that name on their radar and came up blank."

I thanked my friend for the great work that he had done and hung up. Naturally he had told me that he wanted to visit Alaska and when he does, I could show him around. "Sure thing," I told him. If I had a dime for everyone who told me they wanted to visit Alaska, I would have a ton of dimes.

I walked back into the Chief's office and filled him in on what I had learned. "At least we know that we're on the right path, even if it's a dead end. Why else would anyone go to such lengths to hide their identity connecting them to a cell phone unless they had a good reason to do so, meaning they were more than likely up to something illegal."

"I agree," stated Chief Sully. "I would bet a month's pay that reason was a bullet that had your name on it."

"Thanks for the reminder Chief."

"So now we can add that to what we already knew. Albert Shelton got a call from someone in Denver, Colorado, and after getting that call he went and waited for you and fortunately missed his intended target," Chief Sully said wryly. "The time of the call from Denver to Shelton was after you had arrived into town. The call to Denver from Shelton's phone was after you had been shot at."

"You're right." I said to the Chief. "If it looks like a duck . . ."

"We still have to go back to the beginning with the Cranes." Chief Sully reminded me. "I've known Albert Shelton since I first arrived in town. I can't recall him ever going to Fairbanks more than a couple of times a year.

How could he even have an association to Colorado? Whatever that connection was, it seemed to have come out of the blue from all appearances."

"Do you get the idea that Albert was some sort of errand boy in all this?" I asked.

"That certainly makes sense. From what I know of Albert, that would be my guess. But we still need to figure out what *'all this'* is exactly and I pretty much believe all our questions will be answered," the Chief said with a dead serious look on his face.

Chapter 13

Chief Sully and I decided it was time to visit with as many people we could think of who might have known the Cranes. Even though it was evident from the original investigation that Jess and Linda kept to themselves and weren't particularly social, we knew there were places they had to frequent in town and it was reasonable to assume they had contact with several different people.

The Crane's employer checked out during the initial investigation. They owned two similar lodges in the lower forty-eight states and all the businesses were doing well with no hint of trouble. By all accounts, the Cranes were doing a great job. The main office for the corporation was located in Seattle, Washington.

We concurred that it was best to talk with people in town that we knew the Cranes would have been in contact with and the logical place to start was with the trapper who had originally found them.

We located Jerry Smart, the trapper who originally discovered and reported the deaths. He was at his home caring for his dogs.

"Hello Jerry, I'm Jake Rohn, an investigator with the State Attorney General's office from Anchorage."

"Nice to meet you," said Jerry as he shook my hand. "Any word on Albert Shelton?" he asked the Chief.

"Nothing yet; they're still searching," responded Chief Sully.

I figured getting right to the point was best. "Chief Sully and I are doing some follow-up on the Crane case and felt we should speak to you."

Jerry Smart was a direct and no nonsense guy. "I told the other investigators all that I knew. I stopped to visit the Cranes and the door was locked. I looked in the window and I saw them dead. I reported it as quickly as I could make it to town."

I nodded and let Jerry finish his account of what had happened. "I understand Jerry, but I wanted to ask you if there was anything you might have thought of since then that you could tell us. Is there anything you remember that could help us with the case?"

Jerry looked at me for a moment and then answered. "I don't think Jess Crane would have harmed his wife or himself, if that's what you mean. At the same time I can't think of any reason why anyone would want to harm them either. Maybe it was cabin fever like they say. I only knew the young couple a short time. Jess had come to me and asked about the surrounding country. He was interested in doing some fishing and exploring and he just wanted to learn what I knew since he had heard I'd been hunting and trapping around here most of my life. I liked them both, so when I was out their way I would sometimes stop by and visit."

"When had you last seen them alive?" I asked Jerry.

"A week or ten days before finding them dead I'd stopped and visited with them."

I shifted my weight from side to side - damn knee pain when I stood still too long. "Did they seem different to you or did you notice anything odd?"

Without hesitation Jerry replied. "No, they seemed in good spirits to me, as friendly as always."

It was clear to me that Jerry Smart couldn't add anything more to what he had already told investigators months earlier.

Sensing I was done asking questions, Chief Sully told Jerry that we appreciated his time and asked him to let us know if he did think of more.

We left Jerry to his work and drove over to the post office. When we entered the building, the first person we saw was the postmistress, Alice Pratt. Alice came around from behind the counter and gave me a hug. "Well, I was wondering when you were coming by to see me!"

I was wondering how she even knew I was in town. "Alice, you know I would come by and visit. How is Earl doing these days?"

"Earl's at home taking a nap most likely. Since he's semi-retired all he does is nap and fuss at me," Alice said with a smile.

Alice and Earl Pratt were lifelong residents of Alaska and Fort Yukon. I had spent several days working with Alice helping the postal service with controlled deliveries of illegal items that were mailed to the residents of Fort Yukon and surrounding villages. I had grown to love and trust the elderly couple.

"Earl and I were hoping you would have dinner with us before you leave town, unless you plan on sneaking out the way you tried to sneak in."

Without hesitation I replied. "How about tonight, if that's okay with you two?"

"That would be great. What about seven?"

"I'll be there with my appetite," I responded.

"Earl will want to take you on in a game of cribbage if you still know how," Alice said, laughing.

"Oh, I know how and you tell Earl I'm on to his slight-of-hand card tricks!" I laughed too.

It was great to talk with Alice. She and Earl had been as kind to me as my own family since the day I had first met them.

Chief Sully was patient and allowed Alice and me to talk pleasantries for a few minutes. When he noted a pause in the conversation he spoke up. "Alice, we stopped by to ask you about Jess and Linda Crane. We're just following up on their case and thought you might be able to provide us with some insight on them such as who they received mail from, that sort of thing."

"I'll tell you this much," Alice said. "Jess Crane didn't kill his wife or himself. At least I don't believe he would normally do such a thing. Maybe it was cabin fever like everyone suspects, but I don't buy that explanation."

"How can you be so sure?" I asked.

"I know people," Alice explained. "There's no way that Jess Crane would have done what people are saying. I knew the two of them since they arrived. They regularly sent and received mail to and from Canada. It seemed like regular family mail to me. I never saw or suspected anything irregular pass through this office, from them or to them."

I smiled at Alice. "You would certainly know if anything was suspicious, I can vouch for that."

Alice had started cleaning up around the post office lobby as she spoke to us. "Those two kids were as nice and pleasant as they come. A terrible shame their lives were cut short. If Jess did this . . . he had to have gone mad without warning. If someone else did this, those kids crossed the wrong person."

I wondered if Chief Sully felt the same as I did. Alice Pratt hit the nail right on the head with that statement. "Thanks for your help Alice. I'll see you tonight. Oh, how did you know I was in town anyway?"

"Gordy Basil told me. You were on the plane he met the other morning. Gordy is contracted to haul the mail to and from the post office and airport," Alice explained.

The Chief and I said our goodbyes and left the post office.

"Where to next?" I asked as soon as we had climbed into our vehicle.

"How about we talk with the store manager, Marvin Dover?" suggested Chief Sully.

Marvin Dover was the manager of the Yukon River Trader or the *'YRT'* store as it's referred to by the locals. Dover had lived in Alaska for about ten years and in Fort Yukon a bit over a year. I hadn't actually met him but had heard of him through Chief Sully. The Chief seemed to make it a point to know everyone who lived in town, particularly newcomers.

We made the short drive to the YRT and went inside. The YRT was a one stop shopping store for the Fort Yukon residents. You could buy shoes, all types of clothing, food, hardware, fishing and hunting gear, ATVs and parts, electronics and most any household need that arose. At that time of day there were very few customers inside the store. We located Dover in the store office. He was doing what I guessed store managers did most of the time. He was busy working in front of the screen of a desktop computer.

"Hey Dover, do you have a few minutes to speak to us?" Chief Sully asked.

"Sure thing Chief, come on in and have a chair." Dover responded as he stood up and dragged two chairs over by his desk. "Who do you have with you Chief?"

We all three settled down in our chairs.

"This is Jake Rohn," Chief Sully told him. "He's an investigator from Anchorage and is here looking into the deaths of Jess and Linda Crane."

Dover looked over at me and nodded. "How can I help?"

Since Chief Sully knew Dover far better than I, we had decided it was best for him to ask Dover questions. "We're wondering how well you may have known Jess and Linda Crane?" Chief Sully asked.

"Well," Dover began. "I knew the two of them very little actually. They came in the store and bought your run of the mill supplies. Jess did purchase some fishing and hiking gear such as tackle and clothing. I even took him fishing up the Porcupine River once. He asked if he could go out with me on my boat, so we went, in July I think it was. We caught some pike and grayling up a slough about thirty miles upriver."

"How good of an outdoorsman was Jess?" I asked Dover.

Dover looked my way. "I would say he was a bit more than a beginner. He told me he was able to use a small boat from the lodge and do some fishing and exploring that way. He was looking forward to winter so that he could get to more country by snowmachine."

Chief Sully continued with the questions for Dover. "Did either of them ever say anything to you at all that would make you think they were afraid of someone or there was something different in their lives?"

Dover rubbed his chin and looked upward as if he was thinking. "No, the both of them were polite as well as quiet. They always seemed content and were looking forward to making a life here."

More of the same. It seemed as if everyone had the same general impression of the Crane couple.

I stood up and shook hands with Dover. "Thank you for your time, if anything comes to mind please let us know."

Chief Sully and I left the YRT and drove to the only gas station in town, then to the airport and lastly to the local restaurant. We spoke to another half dozen people and we were given basically the same information at each stop. The Cranes were a nice young couple who enjoyed what they were doing; they seemed content and were liked by everyone they met. They generally kept to themselves and Jess had an interest in fishing, hiking and exploring. That would make them the stereotypical Alaskan in my book.

We had spent several hours talking with different people around town. Once again, we hadn't really uncovered any new information. That particular fact seemed to be how this case was proceeding. We returned to the PD after a long day of interviews. It was just after six in the evening and Fanny had left for the day, but Dale Mason was at the office. Dale had the six at night to six in the morning shift - lucky him. Maybe I should consider having Dale stop by the bunkhouse if I couldn't sleep. I liked Dale and having the opportunity to talk with him one on one could be a good thing.

Since the call load for the PD wasn't terribly busy there was usually only one officer on duty at a time. Dale had a radio phone with him. If a resident called the police, Dale could answer the call on his radio. That was a nifty piece of equipment that doubled as a police radio. It saved the city a lot of money not having to pay dispatcher salaries twenty-four hours a day.

All of the police officers, four counting Chief Sully, had their own radio and could monitor the calls and any radio traffic even when off duty. Chief Sully told me it was a great way to keep up with everything that happened on a shift as it occurred. An officer could request backup or contact the Chief whenever needed.

As the Chief removed his coat and gloves he spoke to Dale. "Anything happening around town Dale?"

Dale shook his head from side to side. "Not really. There was a call that came into the office a bit ago about some dogs running loose up town."

"Okay," said the Chief. "Have you heard how the search for Albert is going?"

"No news since I've been here. Fanny didn't mention anything before she left for the day," Dale said as he slid on his coat and then put on a hat and gloves. "I need to go and look for those dogs. You two have a good evening." Dale departed out the front door.

I stood in the front office with Chief Sully. "What do you make of things now after talking with people who probably knew the Cranes the best?"

Chief Sully had a washed out look. "We seem to know that they were a nice couple and that Jess liked to fish and explore the out-of-doors whenever he could. But we knew that much before we started."

"Yeah I agree. Have you asked Kyle Jeffers what he knew about them?"

"Yeah, I did in fact," replied the Chief. "Jeffers had dealt with the couple on a reported domestic dispute. They had a verbal disagreement over nothing specific and they were overheard arguing by some of the lodge guests. Jeffers followed up to find it was just a harmless squabble. This was maybe a month after they had arrived here and began working at the lodge."

"That's right; I recall reading about that in the original report."

"Actually, that's been the only negative piece of information about the couple that has ever come up," said Chief Sully. "Jeffers said he and Jess talked a little about fishing but since he didn't want to be put in an awkward situation, he'd never actually socialized with the Cranes."

"Well Chief, it's late, so I'm gonna head over to the Pratt's' home for dinner. You have a good night and I'll see you tomorrow morning."

As I started out the door I heard the Chief wish me a good night. It would be an awesome night if I could figure this case out!

Chapter 14

Dinner with Alice and Earl was great. It turned out that I didn't recall how to play cribbage very well after all. Earl beat me handily three straight games; one game by an official skunk - which was embarrassing in itself. Their company and a nice hot meal were welcomed with open arms, and in my case the meal was greeted with a wide open mouth.

We visited well into the evening. We talked about cases I had worked with the help of Alice and laughed at some of the funny things we had run across. It was very nice to spend time with good people such as Alice and Earl. I thought about how they would enjoy meeting Whitney and how Whitney would certainly enjoy meeting them.

Alice was always asking me when I was going to find that special lady and settle down. She was fairly perceptive and I believed she knew I had a bad experience concerning a woman somewhere in my past. She was polite enough not to pry. That would be one more reason why I liked Alice as much as I did.

The Pratt's have had a long standing invitation to dinner, my treat, whenever they could make it to Anchorage. Unfortunately the few times they have made it to Anchorage, I've always been away working on a case.

"When are you two going to visit me?"

"As a matter-of-fact I have a training class to attend in Anchorage next month, perhaps Earl will come along and we can see you then," Alice said.

"That would be fantastic! Be sure to let me know when you get to town and I'll make time for you."

Naturally our conversation drifted to the Crane investigation. Earl and Alice had their finger on the pulse of this town pretty good in my opinion. Listening to them repeat things that different townsfolk had said about the Cranes mimicked what we had heard all day. They were a nice couple, kept to themselves and were generally well liked.

"The frustrating thing is that we're no closer to knowing what really happened to the Cranes than we were when I first rolled into town. Actually I would say that we are even farther from the truth than before."

"I know you'll get to the bottom of this," Alice said.

"Thanks for having such faith in my ability."

Dinner and the extended visit with this couple was just what I needed. I was able to relax and enjoy a good meal. It was almost eleven o'clock when I excused myself and made the short, albeit very cold, ride back to my quarters. It was at least twenty degrees below zero outside. The night was clear and I marveled at the number of stars visible in the sky. I didn't believe there was another place on earth where the sky could be so full of stars on any given night. If it hadn't been so cold out, I would've taken a spin around town in hopes of getting a better look at the sky and with any luck, a peek at the aurora borealis.

I've seen the northern lights many times during my five years in Alaska. The colors of the aurora borealis can range from shades of red, green, blue and yellow; or any combination. Breathtaking! They are typically seen the best when it was clear and cold out. Watching the northern lights dance across the sky was certainly magical. I would like to have seen them that night, but just as I had no magic that helped solve this case, there was nothing magical in the sky for me to take pleasure in.

Back at the bunkhouse I stretched out on my bed. I had checked my phone hoping that Mark Dillon had called me and left a message but there was none. I took a minute and sent one of the other investigators from my office a text message asking for an update on Dillon's progress.

My mind was pretty well fried for the day. I'm not sure how long it took for me to fall asleep, but I eventually did just that.

It was two o'clock in the morning at an average bar in downtown Denver, Colorado. A man sat alone in a dark corner of the bar. He was listening to the droning of the juke box as it played some sad country song he didn't recognize - and didn't care to.

"How can people listen to that shit?" he growled out loud, but only he heard his soft spoken words.

The man took out a few dollar bills and tossed them up on the bar. "Hey bartender, play something that won't make us all fall asleep on the bar or cause us to cut our own throats for crying out loud!"

The bartender acknowledged the man with a nod and took the money and then made change from the cash drawer and walked over to the juke box. In a minute's time, the tear jerker of a song ended and was replaced by an upbeat Kenny G jazz tune.

The man grinned to himself thinking how much better that was. He continued to nurse his drink, he was deep in thought.

'Why doesn't he call me back, dammit,' he thought. *'It's been hours now.'*

He remembered a phone call he received on Monday. He'd been led to believe that the Jess and Linda Crane thing was far behind them. He'd thought the case was closed only to find out an investigator was back poking around, Jacob Rohn of all people!

The man, known by some only as *'Marcus'*, stood up. "Jesus fucking Christ!" he groaned. He threw an empty rocks glass into a stone fireplace as he exited the bar and stormed off into the night.

I woke up abruptly and looked over and checked the time. A couple of minutes after four in the morning, four-o-five to be precise. I recalled the nightmare again and shook my head. My heart was racing so fast that I knew it would be impossible to go back to sleep. Not on that night.

I rolled out of my bunk and got me something to drink and sat at the small table and stared blankly into the dark. I had poured a glass of water but wished I had something stronger to calm my nerves. I had been through this too many times. As hard as I tried to suppress the memory of that dreadful night, I realized I had to face it yet again.

I lived in Colorado Springs at the time. This was about eight years after becoming a police officer. I'd been a detective for almost two years when things for me changed forever.

I was living with my fiancée, Tina Bradshaw. Tina was everything to me. Her warm smile and gentle personality complimented me in a way I could never explain, or felt the need to. She was charming and loved by everyone she came in contact with. We'd been together for three years and though we talked about marriage, no date had been set. She had joyfully accepted my proposal. I didn't think it was possible to be any happier than I was at that particular time in my life.

Tina worked for a software developer and she had traveled to Denver for a two day conference. To save money, we'd put her car up for sale so she drove my pickup whenever she needed to go someplace. I was lucky to have an assigned unmarked take home car, so actually we needed just the one vehicle anyway.

Tina had elected to drive home after the long second day of the conference. She was driving south and had just passed Castle Rock when it happened. The official report indicated that at about one-thirty in the morning, Tina fell asleep at the wheel and drove off the road which caused the pickup she was driving to overturn several times, killing Tina instantly.

I was called at precisely four-o-five a.m. I'll never forget my supervisor on the phone. He didn't want to tell me the entire truth straightaway; he tried to break it to me gently and get me to the hospital so that I could be told in person. I knew Tina was dead; he knew that he couldn't tell me anything less than the truth. It was hard enough to take, but if I thought there was some hope only to find out later that she had been killed would've been more agonizing. I just don't think there was a good way to tell anyone such tragic news.

After that, I was fairly useless to everyone and just couldn't get myself back on track. Even now when I get called late at night, I almost always panic thinking I have bad news coming. Everything I did and everything I saw in Colorado made me think of Tina. It didn't take me long to decide that I needed a change.

Though I really liked Colorado Springs, I didn't have anything keeping me there. That was when I made the decision to relocate. I heard that Alaska was starting a special unit of investigators to work for the State Attorney General's office out of Anchorage. I decided to apply and was offered a position with the new unit which I accepted without hesitation. That was the chance for the new start I needed as well as the change of scenery that helped escape the memories that haunted me at every turn. That was more than five long years ago. I felt that I'd left everything behind me except for Tina's memory and that damn nightmare I'd been having for so long.

The only living soul I'd told this story to had been Whitney. About the only time I didn't have the nightmare was when I stayed the night with Whitney. Maybe I should ask her to move in permanently and perhaps the nightmare would stop completely.

Now that Denver, Colorado, had popped up with this current case and brought all that emotion to the surface, I wasn't certain that it was possible to keep the two separated. I was afraid that the intensity of that nightmare would increase and its influence on me would gather strength with each episode. This wasn't a connection I could've ever dreamed of, or wanted.

The best thing for me to do was to take it one day at a time. I had set a course in my mind to continue grinding on the task at hand. All of those old feelings would fade, or at least that was what I kept telling myself.

It was a couple of hours before the Chief was due to stop by and pick me up. I made myself a cup of hot, nice smelling coffee and set it on the table for nothing more than its aroma. I wondered if that's what the term *'aroma therapy'* meant. It worked for me.

I prepared and ate some breakfast and cleaned up my mess afterwards. Then I decided to review the files on this case yet again. As I thumbed through the pages for the umpteenth time, there was one nagging question that I couldn't shake. How was it possible that Denver, Colorado, could be connected to a double murder in the Alaska wilderness?

Chapter 15

"Good morning Sully," I said cheerfully as I crawled into the vehicle. "So how damn cold is it anyway?"

"Twenty-five below," muttered the Chief.

"Wow, in other parts of the world we would be wearing short pants, short sleeves and a straw hat!" I pointed out.

"Yeah and fighting two million people on a daily basis," remarked the Chief. "I want to stop and check the mail."

"Okay, I'll wait in the warmth of this vehicle; it's too damn cold this morning to get out if I don't have to," I smiled.

About a minute passed and I saw the store manager, Marvin Dover, walking up to the window on my side of the vehicle.

I rolled down the window and greeted Dover. "Good morning. Cold enough for you today?"

Dover was dressed well for the weather. He had on winter boots, insulated pants, a hooded parka and gloves. He removed his gloves and held his hands up to his mouth, cupped them together and blew warm air into the space between his hands and fingers. He moved his hands down and away from his mouth in order to talk. "You asked me to let you know if there was anything I thought of and I did. The last time I saw Jess Crane he had stopped at the store to get a few things. We talked briefly but he said to me that there were dangers out there we never knew existed. We had been discussing being out and doing some fishing and hiking. I was kind of busy and had to cut our talk short so I wasn't able to ask him what he meant by that. Maybe it's nothing but I thought I'd let you know. I remembered this after our talk yesterday and I'm glad I bumped into you so fast."

I thanked Dover for telling me what he remembered. Dover donned his gloves, wished me a good day and walked off towards the YRT store. As I watched him walk away I began thinking how great it was for these little clues to keep falling into our laps. The Chief and I needed to talk about this. I thought I knew how our morning would be spent.

As soon as Chief Sully returned from checking the mail I told him about my visitor. "Chief, I just had a visit from Marvin Dover while you were inside. He related to me something Jess Crane said to him that I believe may be important. Let's go to your office. I know there are some things you need to do and I want to sort some things out myself."

"Sounds like a plan," said the Chief.

We drove to the PD in just a couple of minutes. In the small community of Fort Yukon, a person could drive to any location in town in just a couple of minutes. We hurried into the warm building to escape the cold after exiting the comforting warmth of the vehicle. Chief Sully checked in with Fanny before we got down to business. Since I had arrived in town things had been quiet for the police department, with the exception of this case. At the very least we had that going well for us.

I called my office in Anchorage and spoke to one of the office assistants. She told me that something big was happening in Delta. She knew that there had been a shooting involving a Trooper who stopped a vehicle that was suspected of bringing drugs across the US/Canadian border on the Alaska Highway near Tok. The suspect was believed to have been wounded but had fled back toward Canada in another SUV that they assumed had been following the drugs. A huge shipment of marijuana and cocaine had been seized from the vehicle the Trooper had originally stopped. A tremendous manhunt was currently underway in that region of Alaska and across the border into Canada. The FBI and DEA were involved since the drugs had come across the border. It was no wonder I hadn't heard from my boss.

After a few minutes Chief Sully walked into the office I was using and sat down. "The search team believes they've found Shelton's snowmachine under the water but they can't retrieve it. Shelton's body hasn't been located. There's no telling when, or if, his body will ever be found."

When he finished, I related what I had just been told about the events going on in Delta Junction.

"So other than the asshole the Trooper shot, is everyone else okay?" the Chief asked.

"From what I can tell everyone is fine. There's something really big going on there for the FBI and the DEA to get involved just over some average shipment of drugs," I remarked.

Chief Sully grinned. "All we have is an insignificant double murder, but the two of us can handle it."

"Yeah, speaking of handling it, this is what I'm thinking. We have searched the cabin the

Cranes lived in, we have searched the lodge, we have searched Albert Shelton's place," I paused.

"Okay, what's your point exactly?" asked the Chief.

"We've gone over the Cranes' past and nothing has surfaced that would provide an explanation as to why they were murdered. We've spoken to everyone here that knew them or had any contact at all with them and we've spoken to their families in Canada. Still there's been nothing anyone has related to us that adds up to a double murder."

The Chief looked at me. "I still don't get where you're going with this."

"Alice told us that Jess went mad or perhaps had crossed the wrong person. Everyone told us the Cranes were great people. Everyone also told us that Jess liked to explore the wilderness. Just a little while ago Marvin Dover told me that Jess made a statement to him that there were dangers out there that we never knew existed. Maybe we're looking at this from the wrong angle."

Chief Sully was concentrating so hard on what I was saying that I believed I could actually smell wood burning. "You're suggesting that the Cranes saw or found something during their travels that ultimately got them killed?"

"Exactly!" I said excitedly. "I saw some drawings and notes that Jess had made in his journal of areas he'd explored. We've exhausted every other thought or idea on why they would've been murdered, except the possibility that they were murdered over something they found, or maybe they weren't supposed to see or know about."

Chief Sully looked as tired as I felt. "What do you suggest that we do? You talk about a needle in a haystack! This would be a needle in a hundred-thousand haystacks."

"Maybe, but we have Jess Crane's drawings and writings to help us. I say that is where we should start our search."

I located Crane's journal and map among the boxes of evidence and looked at his notes and other entries he had made. It seemed as though he was marking areas on the map that he had an interest in, such as good fishing or camping spots. There were some areas where he had gone hiking that he had marked as well.

"Hey Chief, how about you call Kyle Jeffers in and we let him look at some of this. Since he spends a lot of time out there himself, perhaps he can be of some help," I suggested.

"Yeah, that sounds like a good idea," agreed Chief Sully.

"You know Chief, we had already thought it was possible that the Cranes had seen something or crossed someone that got them killed. Honestly, I can't think of another scenario that fits."

Chief Sully picked up the phone, dialed a number and spoke to someone I believed to be Kyle Jeffers on the other end of the line.

"Kyle will be right in," Chief Sully said as he hung up. "He said he was hoping we would ask for his help with this case all along."

"The more the merrier Chief. I don't think we could get too much help on this case; an extra set of eyes and a fresh perspective may be just what is needed to help us along."

Chapter 16

About fifteen minutes later Kyle Jeffers arrived at the office. Chief Sully brought Kyle up to speed on most of what had transpired so far and what we had hoped he could do to help us. Specifically, we wanted him to look at some of what Jess Crane had written, marked and sketched concerning his explorations of the area and with any luck Kyle could shed some light on what might be there.

"Kyle, you've been out there more than any of us. You spoke to Jess Crane several times as well. We're hoping that you could look at this and possibly see something that might narrow down our search," the Chief explained.

While Kyle was reading through the journal that Jess had kept, Chief Sully recounted events that had occurred around town before and after the Cranes had been killed. He couldn't recall any specific changes in the area or any cases that were out of the ordinary. Things were pretty much as they had always been during his prior years as Chief of Police.

We wondered if Jess had something of value or had found something of value that someone else wanted for themselves. Again, we drew a blank on what that could have been, even if there was something. From all accounts, it was evident that the Cranes had just enough money to get by on and if there was something valuable that they possessed, no one knew what that could've been. Even their families were unable to come up with a single idea. So far if there was a secret, it was just that - a secret.

After an hour or more of thinking, discussing and sharing ideas and combing over the journal and drawings, we were still without any answers. Jess had written mostly about fishing and hiking and that was about it. He really liked exploring.

"Chief, I don't see anything here that would fit what you asked me to look for. It all seems fairly straight forward," said Kyle.

I was looking at a hand drawing Jess had made and compared it to an old grid map. It was apparent that Jess liked to mark good fishing holes and generally noted in his writings how the fishing had been at those particular spots. I noted a circled area on the map and on a corresponding drawing. It appeared to be a hill or cliff bordering the Porcupine River, perhaps five miles upriver from the lodge.

That area was on the north side of the river and it was most definitely isolated. On the hillside opposite of the river, were two circled letters - *'c/o'*. It was fairly faint but it was similar to other notations on the map that marked notable fishing spots as it consisted of a couple letters that had been circled by Jess. This entry was certainly different for two reasons. It didn't encompass any water and there were no other writings by Jess that described the fishing or other significant information about that location.

"I know that place," said Kyle. "It's about the highest hill around and it's actually a steep cliff on the river side. But there's nothing unusual about it as far as I'm aware."

We looked over the remaining notes Jess had made and compared them to the drawings and maps. That particular spot noted on the map where the cliff was located was the only entry that seemed even remotely different from all the others.

"If you think we should check that area out, we can be up to that cliff and back to town in just a couple of hours, no problem at all," said Kyle. "If we get an early start we can check out the entire area Jess Crane covered and be back before dark."

At that stage it was all we had to go on anyway so we decided that was exactly what we were going to do.

"Kyle, we want to leave as early as we can tomorrow. If you can take a map and chart us out a route that will allow us to cover all these areas, that will be a huge help," I said.

"Okay, I can do that. Is there anything more I can help with right now or can I go and start getting my gear together?" asked Kyle.

"That's all I can think of right now. Thanks so much for your help with this. If the Chief doesn't have anything for you I don't see any reason why you can't leave."

"Go ahead Kyle, we'll see you in the morning," echoed the Chief.

Chief Sully and I spent the next few hours reviewing our notes and discussing the chain of events up to that point.

I called Anchorage to get an update on my boss and that case near Delta Junction while Chief Sully went to visit the city manager. There wasn't any additional news from Delta other than that the search was still ongoing for the suspect and his accomplices.

It had been a couple of days since I had heard anything from Mark. Something just felt wrong about not hearing from him. It was an eerie feeling that I had. I suppose I would have worried regardless of what I had been told. No doubt Mark was just as concerned about what I was doing here as I was about what he was up against. Cops tend to get very close to their co-workers, undoubtedly that fueled my uneasiness.

It had been a lengthy and tedious day, so we decided to knock off early and get ready for the trip we planned on taking the following morning. To be honest, I was exhausted.

The man they called *'Marcus'* exited a Denver restaurant. One of his cell phones rang. He recognized the nine-o-seven area code of the caller from Alaska.

"About damn time you called me, you bastard," Marcus immediately shouted into the phone, without giving the caller the opportunity to speak.

Marcus listened to the voice on the other end for about forty-five seconds. By then Marcus was fuming and once more yelled into the phone. "I don't give a shit what you say! We have far too much at stake to just forget it. Listen to me; you screwed this up, so you fix it! Don't call me on this phone again. I'll call you back in two days. If this problem hasn't been handled by then, I'll personally shove a knife into your heart and the heart of every family member of yours I can find! Do we understand one another?" Marcus paused, he waited to hear the caller respond in the affirmative, which he did. "Don't you fucking forget what I said!" and he ended the call and then casually dropped the cell phone down a storm drain after removing the battery.

Chapter 17

Chief Sully and I went to the YRT and I picked up something easy to cook in the microwave. Then he accompanied me to my quarters for a short while and naturally, like a couple of salty cops would do, we hashed over what we had already hashed over a hundred times that day. It still felt as if we were grasping at straws. We were no closer to knowing who was responsible for these murders than we were when I first arrived. Murder cases are tough enough to solve just after they happen. But months later they are even tougher and the success rate drops dramatically. Every tick of the clock that went by decreased the odds of successfully solving this case.

After the Chief departed for the evening I was left alone with my thoughts. I tried to keep my mind occupied and only think about getting ready for the trip we planned for the following morning. I hoped that we would find something, anything that would help us solve this case or at least provide some sort of direction for us to follow. What did the Chief say? A needle in a thousand haystacks! That sounded like a near impossibility when you thought about it that way. That would be a lot of damn hay!

I finished my meal - a frozen chicken dinner; how utterly bland. After a couple of hours of trying to keep my mind occupied with thoughts other than this case, I finally gave up and stretched out on my bunk and listened to music. It wasn't long before I drifted off to sleep. The last few days had really taken a toll on me. I felt twice my age and judging by what I saw in the mirror earlier that day, I looked even older than I felt.

I must have slept better than I had since I arrived in town. Fortunately I didn't have a single dream, which was a good thing since if I had; it would have been that damn nightmare anyway. Finally the alarm went off, which signaled it was time for me to get up and get ready to face another day. *"Holy crap that is one loud alarm,"* I thought, and considered hitting the snooze button and going back to sleep for a few more minutes.

"Why the hell am I choking?" I asked out loud.

I instantly shot out of my bed as though I had been poked with a cattle prod. I immediately realized that it hadn't been the alarm clock that I had heard; that piercing sound was the smoke alarm that shattered the calm night and wrecked my peaceful sleep. The small room was already filling with smoke so I quickly grabbed my phone as I jumped into my boots before I made my departure. As I fled the smoky quarters, I snagged my equipment bag and coat which I had placed adjacent to the door before I had gone to bed for the night. I flung open the door leading outside and sprinted out of the certain death trap. I thought how happy I was that I had slept in sweats and a t-shirt because it would have certainly been a great deal colder if I had been wearing fewer clothes. It was obvious that at least half of the building was already on fire and it was spreading fast. I caught my breath and then wrapped up in my coat and tightened up my boots. Just as I ended a fit of coughing, wherein I was positive that I had actually coughed up a lung, my phone vibrated in my hand. I glanced at the small screen on the front of the phone and noted that Chief Sullivan was calling me. It seemed peculiar that he would be calling me right then.

"Hi Chief."

"You okay?"

"Yeah," I gasped for more air. "But . . ."

Sensing my confusion Chief Sully explained. "Mason called me. He's getting the fire equipment with some volunteers as we speak. He was notified of the fire and in turn called me so that I could check on you. He was outside of town making some rounds and thought it was quicker to call me than to make the ten minute drive to town himself."

"Okay, I get it now," I managed to say, still getting my senses together.

Within about a minute, Chief Sully arrived in his vehicle and slid to a stop close to where I stood. I wasted no time getting into his rig. It was at least minus twenty degrees outside.

"I thought you were a goner," exclaimed the Chief.

"Well, probably in just another minute or two and I would have been."

Within a few minutes a fire truck and an ambulance rolled up on the fire scene. I was led into the back of the ambulance while the fire crew went to work on controlling the fire that by then had mostly engulfed the building. I was uninjured but the ambulance crew insisted I go to the clinic for a thorough exam. I decided to go with them just to shut them up. I knew I was unhurt but they weren't as convinced as I was.

Chief Sully stuck his head in the back of the ambulance. "I've secured the gear you dragged out of the building. I'll stay here until this is under control. Claire will meet you at the clinic and give you a ride back to our place. We'll meet there."

I nodded in acknowledgement and we sped away.

An hour and a half later I was done being poked and prodded by the clinic staff that had finally come to the conclusion that I was okay. I tried telling them that the entire time.

It was great seeing Claire Sullivan waiting for me. She crossed the waiting room and threw her arms around me. She was near tears as she told me how worried she was when Mason called her husband about the fire. "We thought you were done for. I'm so happy you're going to be alright!"

"Don't worry Claire; it'll take more than that to get rid of me." I tried hard to ease Claire's trepidation. "Let's go, I could use something to drink."

We left the clinic and drove to the home that she shared with the Chief. Once inside, Claire poured me a strong drink and we sat at the table in silence.

Within a few minutes we heard Chief Sully coming through the door. He pulled out a chair and joined us at the table. The Chief looked down at my drink. "You may want another one of those after you hear what I have to say."

I drained my glass and asked Claire for a refill. She obliged by going to the kitchen and after a few moments she returned with a drink for the Chief and me.

Chief Sully wasted no time. "Well, the fire chief says that without a shadow of a doubt the fire was arson. The structure is a total loss and the only parts still standing are the bunkhouse walls."

I stared at my drink and listened as the Chief continued. "It seems that whoever set the fire poured a large amount of accelerant along the wall opposite the bunkhouse. I could smell the gas myself; it was that obvious. The fire is basically out but part of the crew will stay behind and make sure it doesn't flare up and no one disturbs the scene before morning."

I looked up. "Either they didn't know what side of the building the bunkhouse was on and just guessed wrong or this was designed to scare me more than to kill me."

Chief Sully took a long drink. "Yeah, that would be my thought too. Mason doesn't know who called it in. It was just a report that the building was on fire. I think he did a great job in how he reacted."

Claire had a worried look on her face. I wondered how often in the last thirty years she had worried for the safety of her own husband and now she was worried for me. Claire was such an awesome lady. I wondered if I would live long enough to find such a wonderful friend and partner.

Chief Sully continued on. "We got great photos that included all of the looky-loos that showed up. Mason checked all the occupied buildings that may have had any view of your building. So far no one saw anything. The call came in just a few minutes past four a.m."

I looked up at the Chief. My face must have turned white.

"You okay Jake?" He asked.

No way! No one knew about that. "Yeah, I'm okay; it just hit me how lucky I was. Twice, in only a couple of days. If there was any doubt that we had stumbled onto something big, that doubt burned along with my bunkhouse and everything in it."

Chapter 18

After a couple of drinks of whiskey and having narrowly escaped a fire, I slept like a rock. I woke up at ten a.m. and found Sully in the kitchen busy cooking what smelled like eggs and bacon. For that alone he was my hero!

Claire had to work and apparently our trip to scout out some of Crane's areas of interest was put on hold. I escaped that fire with my life first and foremost but I also managed to get out with my boots, phone, heavy coat and a bag containing my work files and the like. I only had a few essentials and one change of clothes, a belt and my duty weapon. I needed to get more clothes and some cold weather gear. We still had a mission to do even if I had to beg, borrow and steal what I needed - well, stealing was out of the question but I somehow had to get what I needed.

There was a second mug of hot coffee and containers of cream and sugar on the table. "Thanks Chief," I said after I took a seat.

Sully brought over two plates heaped with eggs, bacon and toast and set one down for me and one for him. "I don't know what the deal is with you and that cup of coffee that you nurse but never drink. I figured you would tell me when you were ready, so I made you a cup."

"Whitney," I said aloud.

"Whitney?" repeated the Chief.

So while we ate breakfast I told the Chief the entire story about Whitney. How we met and how I bought so much coffee but never drank any. I opened up like a book and told him that now I did that thing with the coffee because it made me feel close to Whitney. The coffee smelled wonderful and it soothed me. I continued holding my coffee cup, occasionally stirring the contents, but I never tasted it.

"Sounds like a very special lady. I'd say that you love her already," said the Chief.

"Yeah, I believe you're right about that," I responded. I held back the story about losing my fiancée. "So, what do you think is our next move?" I changed the subject.

"Well," began the Chief. "I say we get together what you need for us to take that ride up the river. We have a machine at the city shop you can use. We just need to get your gear together."

"The YRT has a good selection of cold weather gear so that should be no problem. Now to figure out who is behind this fire?"

Chief Sully nodded in agreement. "I've been thinking on that. I believe that Albert Shelton was involved but never considered that he was the brains behind all of this."

"So, you think Albert ran from us to keep from spilling the beans?"

"That would be my guess. Albert wasn't a leader. He would make a good soldier and do what he was told," explained Sully.

"That means there's at least one other person here who could exercise control over Albert, and that individual tried to burn me up."

"There's no telling how many people could be mixed up in this mess."

"We have Albert and at least one other person involved. You would know if there was someone new in town, so it has to be someone who's been here all along," I said.

The Chief stood and took our plates to the kitchen sink. "Multiple people make a conspiracy, but for the life of me I can't think of a single person or occurrence around here that would begin to support a theory such as that."

"Chief, I think you would have a pretty good idea if things here had changed."

"Well yeah, I haven't seen any spikes in criminal activity whatsoever. At least nothing I'm aware of and we track all categories of crimes and use that information to provide a report to the city manager every sixty to ninety days."

"No doubt if things were out of line you would hear about it."

"Absolutely," Chief Sully returned to the table. "I've thought about this long and hard but I'm no closer to an answer than I was when you first showed up at my office a few days ago."

I was in the exact same boat as Chief Sully. I excused myself from the table and let the Chief know I would be ready in a few minutes to go to his office. The first thing I wanted to do was to somehow remove the target I had on my back. The only way I knew how to do that was to solve this case and put the bastards in jail that were responsible.

After we left the Chief's home we went to the YRT where I was able to outfit myself with the necessary gear for our trip upriver. Afterwards we went to the PD where I made notifications to my office of the attempt on my life as well as the destroyed state property. I requested an arson investigator so that the fire scene could be thoroughly processed. We already knew what the results of that would be.

There was still no word from Mark Dillon. That troubled me.

Chief Sullivan checked on the status of the search for Albert Shelton. There was no news to report. The crews continued their systematic search. They would cut holes in the ice and used drag lines to search for a body and it was a time consuming process. I wasn't sure how long the search would continue.

It was mid-afternoon and I was more or less killing time at the PD. The Chief occupied himself with administrative tasks that he'd ignored the past couple of days. I sat down and made some notes on everything that had happened. I kept hoping that something would jump out at me. I just felt as though we missed something that would help. Naturally, nothing new came to mind as I scoured over all the information amassed during the investigation. Whoever was behind all of this had only drawn more attention to what they were up to and I knew it was only a matter of time before we figured things out. An arson investigator was due to arrive on the next flight into town, so I borrowed a city vehicle and drove to the airport to meet him.

As I waited for the commuter flight to arrive, I marveled at the clear skies and the sheer beauty of the small town. The temperature was well below zero but the sun seemed to warm things up somewhat. I was especially wary of my surroundings, as there had been two attempts on my life in just a few days. You would think that would spoil the beauty. Actually, it made my senses more aware of everything around me and essentially enhanced the grandeur.

Within minutes a twin engine turbo prop airplane glided in for a smooth landing and taxied to a stop. The engines whined and then silence descended as they were shut down and the props fell still. The door to the aircraft opened and I recognized the third passenger who exited as Jim Steel, an arson investigator with the State Fire Marshall's office based in Fairbanks.

Jim had an easy going manner. He looked more like an accountant than a fire cop. He was tall and thin and wore black framed glasses. I swear you would think he sported pens stuffed in a pocket protector in his shirt pocket - the classic nerd stereotype. I knew this man well and had worked with him on several occasions. He was incredibly good at what he did and I was ecstatic that he was tasked with this particular investigation. I was certain that far too many suspects were fooled by his plain and geeky like appearance and confessed their crimes before they knew what had happened.

Jim waited for his two bags to be unloaded from the cargo hold, then retrieved them and made his way over to where I was parked. "Hi Jake," said Jim as he set his bags down by the back of the vehicle and waved to me.

I exited the vehicle. "How long has it been Jim?"

Jim paused to think about it and replied. "Denali, a couple of summers ago, at that hotel fire."

"Yeah, I think you're right Jim. How have you and the family been?"

"Things have been excellent; we had a baby last year. A girl we named Michelle. Being a dad is the greatest."

"Jim, that's fantastic . . . any grey hairs yet?" I asked.

Jim chuckled. "No, but from what I'm told that will happen in about twelve years or so, when she is a teenager."

I laughed as well. "Jim, thanks for getting out here on such short notice. First, I want to take you to the fire scene and then we'll go to the

PD. Chief Sullivan arranged for you to use this vehicle while you're here. The Chief was kind enough to put me up at his house for a while. We can meet up there tonight for dinner and you can fill us in on what you find."

"Sounds like a good plan," Jim said. "Let's get to it."

I took Jim to the burned Fish and Game building and told him what I knew about how the fire happened. Then we went to the PD where Jim was given a copy of the police report prepared by Dale Mason. Jim then returned to the fire scene to work his magic and solve this entire mess, or at least that was what I hoped would happen.

Chapter 19

Shortly after Jim left the PD, my cell phone began to vibrate. That signaled me to the fact that I had an incoming phone call. I was easily amazed by such technology. I glanced at the screen on my phone and was surprised at what I saw. The call was from my boss, Mark Dillon.

"Hey stranger," I greeted Mark.

"Hey yourself, I got all of your messages; you've been about as busy as I have."

"I'm not so sure about that Mark." I proceeded to fill Mark in on the latest developments over the last couple of days. He listened intently as I related the events right up to nearly having been barbecued the previous night.

"Well, maybe you've been just as busy, only in a different way," Mark mused. "You care to hear what I've been up to?"

"Sure," I answered.

"Well," Mark began. "The manhunt for the suspect the trooper shot ended without success.

The suspect and the vehicle he got away in seemed to have fallen off the face of the earth. We're sure it didn't cross back into Canada. We hustled but came up empty on every possible scenario of where that vehicle could have gone. We believe there may have been a third vehicle involved and that the SUV was dumped somewhere, but so far we've not been successful in locating either vehicle. No one has been treated for a gunshot wound as far as we've been able to determine at this point. All that we have is a vehicle full of drugs that would supply the north half of Alaska for a couple of months."

"So why are the Feds so interested in this?" I asked.

"They seem to think this was part of an operation based in Washington State, that's believed to be expanding into Canada and Alaska," Mark explained. "The vehicle seized is leased to a dummy corporation that has been tied to that same drug operation. Drugs are a huge business and that trooper stumbled upon a big piece of that business."

"You had me worried. I'm glad you finally called me back. What more do you need to accomplish there before you're finished?"

"We're wrapping this up. The Feds have pretty much taken over everything as far as the drugs being smuggled over the border. All we're doing now is finalizing the shooting investigation that involved the trooper which was rather straight forward and clearly justified."

"Are you planning on coming out to Fort Yukon?" I asked.

"Yes I am, but I can't make it until late tomorrow or perhaps the following morning," explained Mark.

"That's great. I'll be looking forward to having your expertise here to help us get to the bottom of this case. It'll be good to have an extra person to keep an eye on me to ensure my safety."

"It sounds like you need it."

I went on to explain that we planned on leaving the next morning to check out areas that Jess Crane had marked or noted on his map and in his writings. I told him we had no other idea on how to proceed at the moment anyway, that we were completely out of leads. We hoped the arson investigation could give us some sort of clue as to who could be responsible but we weren't going to hold our breath. We were already certain it was arson, so we knew that would be confirmed. If anyone locally knew something about this, they weren't talking.

Before hanging up I had a question for Mark. "What did you do with Archie before you left Anchorage anyway?"

"Don't worry about him; he's in good hands. I'll see you later tomorrow or the next day. Be careful," and with that, Mark ended the call.

Marcus dialed an Alaska phone number on one of his throw away or burn cell phones. After a couple of rings, someone answered.

"I know I'm calling earlier than I said, but I had to find out what was happening," said Marcus. "Has this situation been handled?"

"Almost," answered the voice on the other end of the phone. "There was a fire last night and apparently Rohn escaped by the skin of his teeth."

"Do I need to remind you what is at stake here?" Marcus interjected.

"It's been difficult, but I have a plan."

Marcus became agitated immediately, and he didn't mind showing it. "I have too much time and money invested in this. You best figure it out." With that, Marcus pressed *'end'* on his phone and disconnected the call and then threw the phone up against a wall with all of his might. The phone shattered into several pieces. He laughed to himself. *"That's an entirely new twist on a throw away phone."*

Chapter 20

It was about seven in the evening when Jim Steel arrived at the Sullivan home.

"We had just about given up on you for dinner," Sully said to Jim when he came in.

"I figured you two chow hounds were waiting for me like one dog waits on another," Jim retorted.

"I think I'll stay out of this and help Claire get the table ready," I said.

"Thanks Chief for the offer of a place to stay the night and for a hot meal," Jim told Sully.

Chief Sully motioned for Jim to follow him. "No problem, Jim. I have three bedrooms and right now one is empty, so you might just as well use it."

After the Chief showed Jim to his room, they both returned to find me sitting at the table with Claire, ready to eat.

We had the best meal of moose roast, potatoes, gravy and green beans. Sully had taken the moose last fall and Claire had grown the green beans in a small garden she had in the backyard. Alaska's growing season was short, but the amount of sunlight was incredible and absolutely perfect for growing an abundance of vegetables.

Claire was one great cook. We enjoyed our meal without shop talk. There were a few humorous stories told but that was as close as it came to conversation about our jobs. That was Claire's only rule: no talking about work allowed at the dinner table.

After finishing our meal we moved into the living room where we did get back to the current business.

"Jim," I began. "I'm guessing your investigation of the fire scene has not only identified who was responsible but why it was done as well!" I jokingly remarked.

Jim looked at me like I was nuts but the serious look on his face quickly evaporated as he realized I was just being a smartass. "It was arson alright; a gasoline accelerant was used. I have some samples that need to be analyzed but I'm sure of the outcome. I know you have a lot of faith in me but at the present time I have nothing to identify a suspect."

"I understand Jim; I was just busting your chops," I said. "I'm just happy you were able to make it up here as quick as you did."

Jim smiled. "You're fortunate to have gotten out alive. That fire was intense and with the gas added to some of the other contents in that building, the fire spread so fast and had so many toxic vapors that anyone caught inside most likely would have been killed from those fumes before the flames had a chance to reach them."

"Thank heaven for smoke detectors!" Chief Sullivan added his thought.

I agreed with the Chief. "So, we're completely certain it was arson and there's no doubt it was meant to take me out."

"This is attempt number two on your life, Jake." Chief Sully pointed out.

"That tells me someone stands to lose something in this investigation. That could mean their freedom or money, or both. But what exactly?" I asked.

"That," began the Chief, "is the key to figuring this out."

We spent the remainder of the evening talking about the case. It had us all scrambling for answers. Normally, in such a small community, someone would be talking and information would find its way back to us. That was one of the frustrating aspects about this case - so far we had piled up the questions but hadn't found any answers.

"I just feel that this involves someone who's not from here and it's easier for their secret to be kept," I suggested.

"Albert Shelton was from here but we're fairly certain he wasn't behind all of this, but perhaps only involved in some way," said Chief Sully.

I nodded in agreement. "Yeah, and the scary part is that he apparently told no one what he was up to. Something about this is very organized."

Jim finally spoke up. "To listen to you both I would think this was about drugs. From what I know, people involved with drugs stop at nothing to keep their business going."

I looked over at Chief Sully.

Sully squirmed a bit in his chair. "We've gone over this. I can't for the life of me figure out how drugs could be involved. There's not an obvious increase in drugs around town and there are no new people in town that I would ever suspect of handling drugs. Not one of my sources has revealed any increase of drugs being brought here or to any of the surrounding villages. I agree it smells like drugs but there's nothing happening that would suggest or corroborate such a theory."

"Yeah, but these kind of guys don't advertise openly what they're doing," which I thought was obvious, but I said it anyway. "Chief, maybe something is going on that just hasn't really surfaced yet."

Sully seemed to mull this over. "You could be right but even so, how could this involve the Cranes?"

"Good question. There's no obvious explanation on how the Cranes could be connected to drugs," I said. "I'll tell you this much, I'm absolutely drained. I'm going to call it a night."

I stood and offered my hand to Jim. "Thanks Jim, for everything. I know you have an early plane to catch in the morning, so if I don't see you before you leave, just let us know when you get the test results back from your samples."

Jim firmly shook my hand. "No problem. I'll be in touch."

With that I excused myself for the night. I wanted to stretch out and think about things and then get ready for the following day's work. The plan was to get an early start on our trip upriver. At this point, the only lead we hadn't yet fully covered was the theory that Jess Crane had stumbled upon something that he wasn't supposed to see, or find, and that cost both him and his wife their life. I didn't have any idea what that could possibly have been but I suspected we would know it if we happened to find it. Chief Sully was absolutely correct, our approach was a long shot, but we didn't have any better options.

I expected that Mark Dillon would arrive in town the following day by late afternoon and I hoped to have something positive to report. Chief Sully and I had put quite a lot of thought and effort into this investigation and it would be helpful to have Mark's assistance in putting everything together and hopefully get this case closed. After thirty or forty minutes of thinking, I decided it was time to call Whitney. It was a bit late in the evening, but I had put off calling her for too long. I selected her number on my cell phone and pressed the call button.

After the second ring a wonderfully familiar voice came on the other end. "Well, hello!"

"Hi Whitney, how are you? I've missed you."

Whitney's voice was quite pleasant, and reassuring.

"I'm good, just worried about you is all," she told me.

"I have quite a lot to tell you about what's been happening. I just don't want you to worry."

"How can I not worry about you Jacob? You go away for days at a time and I'm lucky to get so much as a text message from you. I understand we both have things going on in our lives that take up so much time but I do like hearing from you when you're away. Even if it's just a short text message - I care, so naturally I worry."

I had convinced myself that our relationship was still in a carefree stage and we could easily move into and then out of each other's life without any hassle or expectations. I knew now that we had advanced beyond that point. Knowing it was as hard for Whitney to hear as it was for me to tell her, I filled her in on all the events since I had arrived in Fort Yukon. There was a pained silence on the phone for several seconds after I finished speaking.

"I'm extremely grateful that you're safe but later I know I will be mad at you for putting yourself at such risk," Whitney told me.

"But Whitney, this is my job and you know I wouldn't want to be doing anything else."

We've had a similar discussion a couple of times before. It's wasn't easy, but it did let me know how much Whitney cared for me. She was supportive, but with that comes the worry and I would expect nothing less from her. I'd been fooling myself thinking that everything was fine when Whitney and I were apart. This conversation had most definitely convinced me how deep our feelings had actually become.

"I know it is but I've grown so fond of you. It would break my heart if anything bad was to happen. When do you think you may be coming home? I really miss you!"

"I hope we wrap this up and I'm home soon. Mark has been busy but he should be here tomorrow and that will be a huge help. Maybe we'll catch a break and get to the bottom of everything. This case was almost to the point that someone nearly got away with murder. I know we're close to catching whoever was responsible. I plan to keep on doing what I have been and I'm confident something positive will happen."

Whitney let out a heavy sigh. "That's what bothers me so much. If you weren't so close, people wouldn't be trying to kill you."

That was the one thing that I didn't want to tell Whitney but she was smart enough to figure that out for herself. "There are good people here helping me and looking out for my safety. I'll be fine."

Whitney and I talked for a few minutes more. It was a fairly light conversation. That white elephant was tap dancing all around our conversation. She was worried about me and to be truthful, I was worried too.

"Okay Jacob, you call me tomorrow after you get back from your trip."

"I will."

I hung up the phone and just lay there in the dark room. So many things were running through my mind. Some thoughts were at the speed of light and a few were at the speed of a glacier. Countless questions remained unanswered. There was no way anyone could have seen this coming a few days before, I knew I didn't.

I just needed to rest. The following day would offer a new chance to find something that would put everything into perspective. I preferred to be out actively searching for answers rather than just sitting around hoping someone would come waltzing through the door and confess. That only happened in the movies.

At least there would be three of us going out the following day and that made me feel much safer.

Chapter 21

I was up and rummaging around in the kitchen just before seven a.m. when Chief Sully returned home.

"Good morning Chief," I greeted Sully as he entered the kitchen. "Has Jim already left?"

"Yeah, he wanted to get an early breakfast and then make a final check of the fire scene before he had to catch his flight back to Fairbanks."

I had my cup of coffee and toast in hand, so I moved to the table and sat down. "I received a text from Mark that told me he was on his way to Fairbanks and would be out on one of the last flights later today. It'll be good to have him here; maybe he'll make more sense out of this than we've been able to do so far."

Chief Sully joined me at the table. "We should get ready and get to the PD. I told Kyle he should be ready to go before eight o'clock this morning. If we get an early start we can cover a lot of ground."

"Sure thing Chief. I'll be ready to go shortly."

I finished my skimpy breakfast. We put together some food and water and drove to the PD. Kyle Jeffers met us there and he was ready to go. Kyle had mapped a route for us to follow that covered all the places Crane had noted in his writings. We hoped to find or come across anything that could provide some answers to our questions.

As agreed beforehand, Kyle led the way up the Porcupine River. There had to be something out there. What did Jess Crane mean when he told Marvin Dover that there were dangers out there that we never knew existed?

It was sunrise and the colors across the horizon, coupled with the scattered clouds and the snow covering the landscape, were utterly breathtaking. The colors in the sky were vivid shades of orange and red. The white snow and dark green of the evergreen trees were the perfect foreground for the brilliant sunrise. It was about ten degrees below zero when we started out on our trip. The new gear I purchased was perfect and provided all the protection against the cold that I could have hoped for. The air was calm, which was a good thing for us since any wind at all would have certainly driven down the temperature due to the wind chill.

A few hours passed during which time we stopped at several places that Kyle identified as either fishing holes or hiking trails that Jess Crane had made mention of in his notes or marked on his maps. All we saw at these places was snow, ice and more snow and ice. I had begun to think that this particular trip was nothing more than a sightseeing excursion. We had hoped that we would find something that might help explain or better yet, solve these murders, but so far all we had found were scenic trails and good fishing spots.

After another hour of searching had passed, it had warmed up to about five degrees above zero. Since the day began at below zero temperatures, we welcomed the mercury climbing above the zero mark. We could actually feel the warmth of the sun and that alone was enough to lift the spirits of the entire group. We had stopped for some food and water and discussed our next course of action. I asked Kyle about the hill where *'c/o'* was noted on the map.

Kyle took a break from his sandwich. "I thought we would hit that area on our way back."

"Okay, how much further do we go before we turn back?" I asked Kyle.

"It's up to you and the Chief. We've covered almost thirty miles since leaving town. We've gone as far as Crane mentioned in any of his writings or noted on his drawings."

"Alright," I replied. "Let's head back and check anything that seems interesting so that we can be sure we have been thorough. Chief, are you doing okay?"

"Yeah, I'm good," muttered Chief Sully.

After we finished lunch, we began the trip back towards town but this time we stayed more on the opposite side of the river than on our trip upriver. We followed some trails made by trappers and hunters but found nothing of interest.

Kyle stopped his machine and the Chief and I caught up. "Up ahead is that hill you asked about. From the river side the hill rises up as a sheer cliff but rounds out at the top and continues with a gentle slope down the opposite side. The water has been carving away at that hill for thousands of years."

"We're following you, Kyle," I shouted out as I started my machine.

Within a short time the entire hill had come into view. It rose up to a height of about one-hundred and fifty feet out of the tundra and was the highest point for miles around. On the river side it was a sheer cliff just as Kyle described. The Yukon Flats was called that for a reason - it was flat. There were a few hills that ascended up from the earth for no apparent reason and that was one of those granite filled hills.

We circled the hill on the river side first. When we stopped at the base of the cliff and looked straight up, that was a breathtaking sight. On the other side of the hill there were a few trees and a lot of snow. We followed what I believed to be a trapping trail around the base of the hill. Nothing struck me as something that would have gotten the Cranes killed.

I followed Kyle and the Chief followed me. As we passed the hill, I looked back and saw that Chief Sully had stopped and was looking up the hill. I watched him for a few minutes but he continued looking up the hillside. I circled around and pulled up next to him and stopped the engine on my machine. "What are you looking at Chief?"

The Chief stretched his hand toward me. "Hand me those field glasses you've been using." I handed my Steiner binoculars over to the Chief and he looked through them at a spot further up on the hill. I looked up there myself but couldn't really see anything of interest. Chief Sully handed the glasses back to me. "About a third of the way up, next to that biggest spruce, does that look like a trail to you?"

I looked at the area the Chief had pointed out. "You could be right Chief."

"The shadow there was different and it caught my eye," Sully explained.

By then Kyle had noticed that we were no longer following him and he had circled back and stopped his machine next to Chief Sully and me. "You guys find something?" Kyle asked.

"Not sure," I answered. "There seems to be a trail up there. Looks sorta interesting so I think we should check it out since we're here."

Kyle and I started up toward the trail on foot. The Chief stayed with the machines. The snow was a bit deep and breaking a trail up the side of the hill was tough but the slope wasn't too bad. After a couple of hundred feet up the slope we arrived at the big spruce the Chief had referred to. There was a trail to the right of the spruce that went on down the hill following the contour and slowly descended toward the river. That path could've been a game trail but it appeared to stop at a huge boulder at the base of the spruce tree. Odd!

"Find anything?" Chief Sully shouted up.

I looked at Kyle. "What do you make of this? A trail that stops right here." I reached out and kicked the boulder next to the tree.

The look on my face must have been priceless. I kicked the boulder with my toe and it moved to one side about a foot. *'It wasn't a real rock!'* I wasn't sure what it was but I would describe it as being similar to one of those fake boulders they used in the movies.

"What the!" I exclaimed as I pushed the faux boulder to the side and exposed an opening of about four feet across and maybe three feet high. "A cave?"

Kyle had an odd expression on his face too. "A cave! Wow! There could be an animal in there, I'm not going in."

I yelled down to the Chief to come up and see what we'd found. Within a few minutes Chief Sully joined us at the cave opening. It took a couple of minutes more for him to catch his breath.

"Chief, this trail seems to come from around the hill on the river side and ends here at this fake boulder. Behind this boulder is a cave opening. This has to be the *'c/o'* on Crane's notes," I explained.

"Do you think this is an animal cave?" asked the Chief.

"That's what Kyle said, but a fake boulder in front of it? That doesn't add up. This is a place someone is trying to hide from view. This could be the needle we've been searching for."

With that, I dropped down on my knees and aimed a light into the opening which extended a couple of feet at which point it opened up into a large cave. There appeared to be some furniture in the cave, but I couldn't see much as some type of tarp or canvas partly covered the opening on the inside of the cave. I shouted out and threw some stones into the black void. There was no response at all.

I stood up. "Okay guys, I'm going in - there's something in there."

I fell back to my knees and crawled through the opening and into the cave. I held my flashlight pointed forward in one hand in order to see what was in front of me. The way the entry was blocked and there weren't any tracks visible, I didn't believe I would find an animal in the space. As I cleared the entrance I found myself in a cavern a little over seven feet high and maybe ten feet deep and just as wide. This was no ordinary cave. Wooden shelves had been built along the walls; there was an old wooden table and oil stove.

The shelves were well stocked with bottles of alcohol and bags of what I suspected to be drugs. Though at the moment there was no one about, the cavern had both the look and feel of a place that wasn't abandoned but rather infrequently visited. There was no cot or bed which indicated that it was used more for storage than a long term campout spot. Something about the room gave me the impression that it had recently been used, but it was cold. The stove had a pipe, which I assumed was routed out the cave opening when it was lit.

This had to be what Jess found that got him and his wife killed.

"Hey guys, you have to get in here and see this," I shouted toward the cave opening.

I was engaged checking out the shelves full of drugs when suddenly I froze. There was a bone chilling click behind me, close to the back of my skull. Instinct kicked in and my hands shot straight up in the air. I slowly turned to discover that I was right. There was no mistaking the sound made when the hammer of a gun is cocked back into the firing position. Click!

With hands held high and my own weapon covered by my coat, I found Kyle Jeffers staring at me over the iron sights of his weapon. The barrel of that handgun looked large enough for me to stick my fist into. What I really wanted at that moment was the chance to stick my fist through Jeffers' face.

"Dammit Kyle, what the hell are you doing?"

"Shut up Rohn, it's you or me and it's not going to be me. I can guarantee that! Turn around. I had to get rid of Jess Crane and his wife because of his snooping around and finding my cave and you're next!" Kyle screamed.

I slowly turned around and wondered why he hadn't shot me yet. Maybe there was a chance I could get out of this. He was thinking it over or contemplating what he should do. When someone hesitates that means they are unsure or unwilling. Either could be good for me. Maybe he needed to get instructions from someone. What did he do with Chief Sully? I didn't hear a gunshot or any sort of scuffle. A thought came crashing over me like a rogue wave crashing over a breaker wall. This couldn't be happening! Was Chief Sully behind all of this?

"What did you do with Chief Sully?" I asked. I wanted to get Kyle talking in order to buy some time so that I could come up with a plan.

"Shut the hell up," responded Jeffers. "Just don't you worry about the Chief," and then my world went dark as Kyle brought the butt of his gun down hard onto the back of my head and I fell to the ground.

Chapter 22

I woke up with a raging headache. How long had I been unconscious? Where was I? After lying on the cold ground for who knows how long, my entire body ached. Everything came rushing back to me. The cold truth of it all - just a heap of frozen lies littered about.

Kyle Jeffers attacked me. Where the hell was Chief Sully? There was no way that the Chief could be a part of this mess. He would never have pointed out that trail leading to this cave if he was. We could've driven right by this place and I would never have been any wiser.

I was handcuffed and they were biting into my wrists behind my back and my feet were bound together. The ground beneath me was solid, cold and dry which meant that I was probably still in the cave. It was dark and cold inside the cave. I thought I felt something on the ground next to me. Chief Sully perhaps? I not only hoped it was the Chief that I sensed, but I prayed he was still breathing.

I remained still for quite a long time while I listened for sounds. I tried to determine if I was alone. I wanted to get my bearings and come up with a plan to extricate myself, and the Chief, from this dilemma. Other than being cold and having a massive headache, I believed I was unhurt. I knew I had a handcuff key concealed on the inside of my belt at the small of my back, something I had started doing back during my early patrol days. With so much cold weather gear on, it would be hard work just getting to that key.

Where did Jeffers go? How soon would he return and would he be alone? What was Jeffers' part in this? Had Mark arrived to town and was frantically trying to locate us? Was help on the way? Even if someone had started looking, how could they ever find us? My mind raced out of control with so many questions.

I began the slow and laborious task of pulling up my heavy coat and pulling down on my insulated Carhartts in order to reach that key. I thought I heard a low moan and some breathing on the ground near me. I lay still and listened but all I heard was silence. I couldn't tell how long I'd been there and wasn't sure if the darkness was caused by that blockage across the cave's entrance or by nightfall. I assumed that I was in the same cavern where I had been knocked unconscious by Jeffers. I prayed that Sully was there with me and that he was alive.

I was very grateful for two things at that moment. First, that while at the police academy we had actually practiced getting out of handcuffs, and second, that I hadn't been carrying hinged cuffs. These chain style cuffs on my wrists allowed for enough hand movement so that I could get at that concealed key. Hinged cuffs all but eliminated the ability of a person to move their hands. Now that I thought about it, there were a few more things that I was thankful for. One was the habit of carrying that spare key and the other was the game we often played at parties where we handcuffed each other and the winner was the one who could get out of their cuffs the quickest. I couldn't even remember what we won. Cops and parties, we did some bizarre shit. Maybe I would win my life.

It seemed like it took me forever to retrieve that hidden key from under my belt. With the key tightly secured in my hand, I then worked my hands to the front of my body. My feet were bound together but I managed to get my hands to my front by rolling onto my side and pulling my knees up to my chest and then working my hands down and around my backside and then down and around my feet. Not an easy task but I was motivated by the fact that I didn't want to lie there and freeze to death. After I accomplished that, getting the cuffs unlocked with the key was rather simple. Once I had my hands free, I could reach the duct tape that bound my feet. The tape peeled away easily.

I had a small penlight in one of my front pockets. Once I retrieved it, I turned the light on and cast the beam around the darkened room. Chief Sully was on the ground not far from me and appeared bound as I had been. A thin streak of blood ran down his right cheek, but other than that he appeared to be unhurt. His breathing was steady and strong.

There was an oil lamp on the table. When traveling out in this unforgiving country, it was always wise to carry emergency supplies on your person - including matches. I had some emergency matches in one of my pockets which I used to light the lamp since I considered our plight an emergency. As the light danced about the small space I turned my attention to the Chief.

He moaned softly as I removed the hinged cuffs from his wrists. Had I been wearing hinged cuffs myself, I might still be on the ground wondering if that was the Chief instead of helping him. I removed the duct tape from around his feet and legs and then turned him over onto his back. He moaned again as I rolled him over but I saw that he had a large gash on the right side of his head. I tore strips from the t-shirt I was wearing and constructed a makeshift bandage around the Chief's head. His eyes flickered open but I believed he had suffered a severe concussion. I had a huge bump on the back of my head but didn't believe I was injured nearly as bad as Chief Sully.

My weapon and phone were gone. I checked the Chief's pockets and both his phone and weapon were gone as well. Not that our phones would have helped us but having a weapon would have at least been comforting. I noted that it was getting dark outside as I crawled out of the opening of the cave but was unable to see the machines where I knew we had left them. I pulled the fake boulder back over the entrance and crawled back inside the room. We had no supplies, the machines were gone and we were miles from town. No one except Jeffers knew where we were. I suspected Jeffers was either headed for the Canadian border or was back in town spreading some tall tale about what happened to the Chief and me.

I knew that if I kept the opening of the cave covered, the heat from the lamp alone would at least keep us from freezing. The gravity fed oil drip stove wasn't working correctly for some reason and I was unable to get it lit. My stash of matches was limited, so I gave up trying to fire up the stove. I found a tin pan and melted snow over the flame of the lamp. There was plenty of snow, so we at least had ample water. I knew that eating snow wasn't a smart idea in a survival situation. I was glad I had a way to melt it - the water would sustain us for a while. The Chief moaned each time I tried to move him but I managed to get him to drink some water.

Our predicament was dire and we were most certainly in for a long night. I sat back and took in the contents of the cave. There were sets of shelves on each of the cave's walls except the wall where the entrance was located. There appeared to be perhaps a hundred or so bottles of liquor on about half of the shelves. The remaining shelves contained bags of drugs. Lots of drugs! There was packaged marijuana, some cocaine and what I believed to be heroine. There were pills that I couldn't identify right off hand. This was obviously no small time operation. Honestly, I had seen more drugs than what was in that cave only one other time. When I was a patrolman in Colorado, I participated in a huge drug bust at an obscure airfield just outside of Colorado Springs that netted a plane load of the illegal substances.

It all seemed pretty clear now as to what was going on. Kyle Jeffers and someone else, I assumed to be in Denver, had found a way to bring drugs into Alaska through the back door. That meant they brought the drugs across the border from the Yukon Territory, possibly out of Old Crow, and then filtered them throughout

Alaska. Jeffers had to be the man on this end of the operation and was in charge of getting the drugs to a hub location, probably Fairbanks, and from that point they could spread them over the entire state.

I knew that the Porcupine River originated in Canada, in the Yukon Territory. The river flowed north, then turned west, and flowed right by Old Crow in the Yukon Territory and continued west and crossed the Alaska/Canada border. The river continued to flow west until it dumped into the Yukon River at Fort Yukon. The distance between Fort Yukon and Old Crow had to be more than two hundred miles.

In order to open up oil exploration, mining and tourism in Canada, a new road had been built that split off of the Dempster Highway north of Dawson City in the Yukon Territory. That road went all the way to Old Crow where it ended. I knew this because the previous summer I had the chance to drive to Dawson City and continued north on the Dempster Highway and visited Fort McPherson. I was surprised when during that visit I learned of this new road. I didn't have the time to travel it, but remembered thinking that the scenery would be amazing.

I assumed that Jeffers brought the alcohol in from Fairbanks and probably enlisted Albert Shelton to sell and distribute it to surrounding dry villages. Fort Yukon was wet but the cost of alcohol was fairly high and sales were heavily monitored to help prevent alcohol from being taken to surrounding dry communities. Bootlegging could be a lucrative business.

It was impossible to man every mile of the Alaska/Canadian border because so much of it was remote and inaccessible. Where the Porcupine River crossed the border between Canada and Alaska would be one such location. Residents of Old Crow and Fort Yukon were related by history and tradition as well as family ties. They've been traversing between the two towns at will since the communities were first established. The brilliance of this plan was that all the processes and systems were in place to identify and prevent drugs going out of Fairbanks to the villages, not the other way around.

Jess Crane had stumbled onto something that signaled the end for him and his wife, and we had done the same. I somehow had to survive until morning and find a way to get the Chief and me out of there before Kyle returned to finish us off.

Chapter 23

The final inbound flight of the day landed at the airport in Fort Yukon. It was four-thirty p.m. as Mark Dillon exited the plane and entered the terminal where he thought someone would meet him. He tried calling Rohn but received no answer. Not sure what to do, Mark talked one of the cargo handlers into giving him a ride to the PD. He thanked the young man for the lift and gave him a ten dollar bill for his trouble.

It was late afternoon when Mark entered the building. He walked into the main office and confronted Fanny. "Hi, I'm Mark Dillon. I work with Jacob Rohn."

Fanny rose and shook Mark's hand. "Very nice to meet you Mark. Those guys aren't back yet. I expect them any time."

Mark took a seat near Fanny's desk. "Jake told me about their trip upriver to look for anything that Jess Crane might have stumbled upon. I expected they would have been back by now based on what I was told. Did Jake tell you I was coming to town?"

Fanny shook her head. "No he didn't. I guess he thought they would be back in time to meet you himself."

Mark thought about that for a few moments and decided Fanny was probably right. Jake most likely didn't want to let anyone know that he was coming to town. But where in the hell was Jacob Rohn?

At that moment Dale Mason came through the door. "Hey guys, what's up?"

Dale focused on Mark but Fanny spoke up first. "This is Mark Dillon. He works with Jacob Rohn. Mark, this is Dale Mason, one of our officers."

"Hello Mark, how was your trip?" Dale asked as he extended his hand.

"It was good; thanks for asking. I'm waiting for Jake and the Chief to return from their trip upriver," Mark said as he rose to exchange handshakes and then sat down again.

Dale had a quizzical look on his face. "Didn't Kyle Jeffers go with those guys?"

"Yeah, he did," Fanny answered.

"I saw Kyle's snowmachine in front of his house a short while ago. I assumed they were back. Come to think of it, I haven't seen the

Chief's machine anywhere, but maybe he went straight home. Did he check in?" Dale addressed Fanny.

"Dale, let's go see Kyle Jeffers. Maybe he can tell us where Rohn and the Chief have gotten off to." Mark stood and turned to Fanny. "Fanny, call Chief Sullivan's cell phone and let us know if you reach him. Here's my card, it has my cell phone number printed on it if you need to reach me."

Mark and Dale got into a patrol vehicle and drove to Kyle's place. They arrived and exited their vehicle just as Kyle was coming out of the front door of his house.

"Hey Kyle," started Dale. "We . . ."

That was all Dale got out of his mouth before Kyle drew a weapon and shot him at almost point blank range. Dale fell to the ground and was motionless.

Mark dove for cover behind the front end of the patrol car. Kyle continued around the front of the car with his weapon at the ready. Mark was pulling his weapon from its holster even as he dove for cover. As soon as he saw Kyle's head clear the front of the car, he squeezed off one shot that struck Kyle in the center of his face. The forty caliber slug exited the back of Kyle's head. He was dead before his body began to slump to the ground. Mark pulled his cell phone from his coat pocket and dialed nine-one-one. He wasn't sure if it would work but it did.

Fanny answered the phone on the first ring.

Mark began shouting into the phone. "Get an ambulance to Kyle Jeffers' home, Kyle and Dale have been shot."

When Fanny repeated and understood what Mark requested, Mark hung up the phone and went to Dale's side. He had a wound where a bullet had entered his left shoulder and exited out his back. Mark thought the wound was high enough on Mason's shoulder that perhaps it missed vital arteries near the heart. Dale was breathing well enough but wasn't conscious. Mark had a handkerchief folded up in his coat pocket. He took that out and pressed it onto Dale's wound in an attempt to stop or at least slow down any blood loss. From his vantage point at Dale's side, Mark was able to see Kyle Jeffers lying flat of his back and staring blankly upward. He'd seen many dead bodies in his time and Kyle Jeffers was certainly a dead body at that point. *"Serves the bastard right,"* thought Mark.

Within minutes, the whine of an ambulance siren broke the silence and then the vehicle arrived and came to a stop behind the patrol car.

EMTs rushed out and took over Mark's task of attending to Dale. Mark reached for his cell phone and dialed Jacob Rohn's number. "Pick up your phone dammit, what sort of hell have I walked into?" Mark muttered as Jake's phone continued to go unanswered.

Chapter 24

Dale Mason was gently placed on a stretcher and then loaded into the ambulance and taken to the clinic. The word was that he should be fine but he was being prepared to be flown by a medivac flight to Fairbanks. The regional clinic wasn't prepared for major surgery and since there was time to do so, taking him to Fairbanks was best.

Mark Dillon was in a unique situation. He had protected the scene in front of Jeffers' home after removing Jeffers' body. With the help of Fanny, he hired a guard to keep Jeffers' place and the shooting scene secured. Mark had made a call to his office and requested help in the form of an additional investigator and crime scene specialist. Help wouldn't arrive until the following morning. With Jeffers dead, Mason shot and on his way to Fairbanks, the Chief missing and Jacob Rohn presumably with the Chief, Mark was the lone law enforcement presence that remained in town. The fourth and remaining member of the police force had been out of town on vacation for the past two weeks and wasn't scheduled to return for another week.

Mark returned to the PD and discussed the situation with Fanny and enlisted her aid in formulating a plan. Fanny called in Greg Sharp, the fire chief and search and rescue leader for the district. With Greg's help, the town was searched and it was determined beyond any doubt that Rohn and the Chief were not there. The searchers returned to the PD and awaited additional orders. After the events that had just transpired, none voiced the unthinkable, but the thought and fear was still present. There was the possibility that even if Rohn and the Chief were found, they could already be dead.

"Greg, I know you're overseeing the search for Albert Shelton but I need your help to search for Chief Sullivan and Rohn. Can I count on you and a couple of guys to be ready to launch a hasty search as soon as possible in the morning? I'm calling in a Civil Air Patrol aircraft to overfly the area. We need to find them quickly but it's getting too dark to launch a search now," Mark explained.

"You got it. Fanny explained what their mission was and I suspect they are somewhere close to the Porcupine River corridor. A search area as much as fifty miles upriver and back should reveal something for us to go on, even if we don't locate them. If we can find their trail, we'll find them," Greg said with confidence.

Mark looked over a map Greg had spread out on the counter. "Thanks Greg, I know you'll have a satellite phone with you. Can you check in every hour or so in order for us to chart your progress?"

"Absolutely, I can do that," Greg responded. "We'll launch before daylight so I'm going to go and get myself and a couple of guys ready. Should anything change let us know."

"Will do Greg, thank you," said Mark.

With that, Greg Sharp left the office.

I woke up and was relieved that the longest night of my existence was finally over. Well, at least the second longest night. I checked on Chief Sully. He had stirred often during the night but hadn't awakened, which worried me. His breathing had become a bit erratic and shallow and he was hot with a fever. I'd been afraid to sleep in fear that Kyle Jeffers would return but instead managed to catnap on and off - out of necessity. If Jeffers showed his ugly mug, I had a surprise for him in the form of a wooden club that I'd found in the cavern. I had made a plan of sorts. There are lots of rules about what to do and not do when you're lost or stranded. This situation was fairly unique and I wondered what rules would apply. I climbed out of the cave and made my way down the hill to where we had parked our snowmachines when we originally stopped to investigate the trail. I looked down the trail in the dim light of the cold winter morning and about two hundred feet away I saw the back ends of two snowmachines sticking out from under some low brush.

"Sweet!" I thought as I made my way to the machines. My elation quickly faded as I saw that neither machine had a key. With herculean effort I pulled the machines a few feet back and up onto the trail and then opened the hoods. No key was only part of the problem. The spark plug wires had been removed and the drive belts were cut. These things were nothing more than gigantic paper weights. It would be impossible to get the engines to start, and actually driving them would be out of the question.

I climbed back up to the cave and crawled inside. What could I do in order to give Chief Sully and myself a better chance to survive? If there was going to be any search, I would guess it was underway already. It didn't matter what Jeffers had told everyone, there would be people coming out to retrieve our bodies at the very least. I didn't want to leave the Chief alone and with no transportation, I decided against trying to make it to town on foot. I needed to make our location more visible. I had thought about it and my mind was made up as to what I could do in order to accomplish that.

After checking the Chief I exited the cave and returned to the machines where I opened the gas tank on mine. Peering down into the tank, I estimated it was about half full of gas. With much effort, I managed to turn my machine up on its side and propped up against the Chief's machine. Gas gushed out onto the ground and onto the Chief's sled. I took off my gloves and fumbled in my pocket for another one of my emergency matches, struck it and tossed it into the gas that had poured from my machine. Instantly, both machines erupted in a ball of flame and thick black smoke. Beautiful, thick black smoke! Talk about putting all your chips on one number and rolling the dice!

I stood back and watched the smoke curl up into the sky for several minutes. If anyone was looking, they could see this from miles away. Now all I could hope for was that a search party was out and that they were close enough to see this thick smoke. It was full daylight by now and clear as a bell.

Within thirty minutes I heard the drone of a single engine plane. The plane was flying up the river and seemed to be heading directly for the smoke from the burning machines. I positioned myself about fifty feet from the flames and stood well in the open and watched as a Cessna flew directly over me and banked to come back around for a second pass. I waved my arms as the aircraft made another overhead flyby. As the plane was almost directly above me, I saw the universal signal from the pilot that he had seen me. The plane's wings dipped side to side.

On the third pass a passenger in the plane dropped a package that landed near to where I stood. A bright orange colored streamer was tied to the package which aided in my locating it in the snow. I found and opened the parcel which contained some water, energy bars and a radio. As I got the radio out I saw that it was on and the volume was turned all the way up. A voice was calling to me from the speaker of the radio.

It was the booming voice of the plane's pilot that shattered the morning cold. "CAP aircraft to ground personnel."

I keyed the push to talk button on the radio. "This is Jacob Rohn."

"Rohn," the pilot began. "Give me an assessment of your situation."

"I'm okay but I believe Chief Sullivan has a severe concussion. He's been unconscious since yesterday and his breathing is becoming labored and he's also running a fever. The supplies you dropped are all we have."

The pilot quickly responded. "Your position has been passed on to Fort Yukon base. A ground search team is already in the area and medical assistance has been requested."

I was elated beyond description. "Thank you. I will stand by on this channel."

I returned to Chief Sullivan and found that his condition remained the same. I had finally lit the oil stove and positioned the stack to run out of the cave opening. It was much warmer inside the small space. I hoped the warmth would help to improve the Chief's condition or at least prevent him from becoming worse. When I inspected the stove originally, I had missed seeing a valve on the back of the oil canister attached to the stove. Opening that valve had released the flow of oil into the stove and enabled me to get it lit and the resulting heat made a world of difference.

It seemed like an eternity passed by before I heard the faint sound of approaching snowmachines. In reality I learned it was less than an hour since I had been spotted by the search plane. I crawled through the small opening and stood outside the cave and was able to wave down Greg Sharp and the two other riders with him as they approached my position. Greg scrambled up the hill to where I was waiting. "I'm so happy you guys are here. I'm afraid Chief Sullivan is severely injured and is in need of medical attention right away."

The rescue team went straight to work. Greg had a medical bag with him and was able to give the Chief medication that helped his breathing and reduced his fever. He wrapped the Chief's head wound and immobilized his neck and spine. One of Greg's team pulled a sled type stretcher up the hill. We placed the Chief inside the stretcher and secured him. We then slowly lowered him down the hill, taking care not to aggravate his injuries. The search team had two sleds that were pulled behind their machines. The contents were combined and piled onto one sled while Chief Sullivan was placed onto the other sled. In less than an hour we were on our way to Fort Yukon.

Greg and his team were professionals at what they did. They worked quickly and in harmony. I rode with Greg on his machine for the trip back to town.

"We'll be back in about an hour, maybe a little more," Greg said as we started back.

"Be wary of Kyle Jeffers," I yelled to Greg over the sound of his machine.

"No worries there, unless of course he comes back as a zombie," Greg replied.

In all of the excitement and amidst the concern and care of the Chief and our departure, I hadn't asked Greg anything about what was going on in town. We were focused on getting the Chief out of there and to the clinic. Kyle Jeffers was dead! Finally, maybe this was over.

The trail was mostly smooth, but we still had to take it slow with the Chief. We came to the same meadow where I had stopped on the first day I arrived in town. That seemed so long ago. Albert Shelton had tried to end my life that day. I couldn't help but think that if they had kept their cool, I would've left town and the Crane case would've been closed for good.

We traveled for about five more minutes and I could see the clinic come into view at the edge of town. Now we could get Chief Sullivan the medical attention he so desperately needed, I felt relieved and even elated. As we pulled up to the clinic I saw several people filing out of the entrance. Among them was Mark Dillon. I couldn't recall the last time I felt this relieved to see him. Clinic personnel surrounded the Chief and within a few short moments they had him transferred to a gurney and wheeled him inside.

I turned to Mark. "I'm not sure who has the most questions, you or me."

Mark nodded. "You know how to make things interesting."

"I do at that," I remarked.

Mark started toward the clinic. "Let's get you checked out first."

Chapter 25

For the second time that week I was thoroughly examined at the clinic. To me, the more pressing matter was Chief Sullivan and his condition. Come to find out he had a severe concussion as I originally thought. Everyone believed he would be fine, but he needed a few more tests and to be under observation for a couple of days, so he was flown to Fairbanks. His wife, Claire, went to Fairbanks with him. I was medically cleared; just a lump on my head plus a few scratches and bruises. Nothing too bad; I've been through a great deal worse. Everyone had always told me that I was hardheaded. Now I knew that they must have been correct in that observation.

A team that consisted of two investigators and a crime scene technician showed up later that day. They were tasked with investigating the shooting scene that involved Mark and assisted with tying up the loose ends regarding the Crane case.

Chief Sully had regained consciousness and I spoke to him before he was flown to Fairbanks. He said I owed him a great deal for getting him into such a messy case. At least he and Claire gave Mark and me the key to their home so that we had a place to stay.

That evening I sat at the table at the Chief's house. I had my customary cup of coffee in front of me.

Mark joined me at the table. "I didn't know you drank coffee."

"I don't; it's a long story," I responded.

"We pretty much have all this put together now," Mark said.

I nodded and listened to Mark's account.

"Well, it seems that Kyle Jeffers was in Alaska exploring and poking around as he liked to do and discovered that cave. He came up with a scheme as to how he could run drugs across the Canada border and then on to Fairbanks. Or, it was possible that his trip up here was for the sole purpose of finding a way to move the drugs across the border and such a hiding place was the answer. He conveniently talked his way into a job with the Chief of Police."

I stirred and blew on my coffee some more. The strong smell did me a world of good and Whitney was definitely on my mind.

I added my thoughts to Mark's explanation. "It seemed like a difficult route to take - but the payout could be remarkable. Once he worked out the logistics, I would guess the upside for the business was worth the hassle. A couple of locals slipping back and forth between Old Crow and Fort Yukon wouldn't raise suspicion. There's a strong connection between the two communities."

"We found a few recent calls on his cell phone to and from Denver, just like Albert Shelton had on his phone," Mark added.

"Yeah they both seemed to be tied to this *'Marcus'* but all the numbers for Colorado turned out to be from prepaid cell phones purchased with cash and are untraceable. Kyle had a security firm in Denver listed as a place of employment on his application the Chief had on file. That firm seems legit but the owner had little to no information on Jeffers. We have him linked to Denver in more ways than one," I paused.

Mark picked where I left off. "Jeffers must have made a contact that had access to the drug trade while he was in Denver and then used Albert Shelton to help him locally. I doubt Jeffers told Shelton much about the entire operation, but had him sell alcohol and likely used him as a contact for whoever was transporting the drugs from Canada."

I nodded. "Makes sense to me. Jeffers was stockpiling the drugs in a place he felt was safe and known only to him. His trips out of town were for that purpose, under the ruse of hunting and fishing. Hell, who would think it necessary to check a cop that was transporting a prisoner to Fairbanks or traveling for any reason. Jeffers had the perfect setup and cover to transport the drugs to town and sell them."

My mind wandered while I paused to stir my coffee. Once again I thought of Whitney and Archie. "Jess Crane stumbled across that cave and was scared shitless over what he found. I would guess that he decided to confide in Jeffers since he knew Jeffers was a cop but Crane and his wife wound up dead for their trouble. Jeffers admitted to me that he killed the Cranes."

"The drugs alone were valued at over one-hundred-fifty-thousand dollars. I don't know about the alcohol but it seems clear the drugs were coming across the border by way of the Porcupine River from the Yukon Territory." Mark went on to explain.

"Now the Feds need to be brought up to speed. They'll certainly be interested in this. So far we can't link a single person to this other than Kyle and Albert locally, both of whom are dead and a *'Marcus'* somebody in Denver. As it stands now, the Denver connection will remain anonymous but maybe the Feds or authorities in Denver will come up with something."

I picked up my coffee and tried a taste. "The only loose end is the source of the drugs. They are presumably from Denver and are brought into Alaska by boat in the summer and snowmachine in the winter. We may never connect that final dot."

Mark eyed me like I was nuts. "Oh, that reminds me. Albert's snowmachine was recovered from that open lead he drove into on the river. After tomorrow the search for Albert's body will be suspended if it's not found."

I shook my head at that news. "Mark, is Archie okay?" I've been thinking of him a great deal. Well, about both Archie and Whitney actually.

"Yeah, he's fine; I guess you'll see him late tomorrow or early the next day. The troopers flew two guys out here to hold down the fort . . . the fort; that's a good one . . . until the Chief can get back and get things covered out here." Mark smiled from ear to ear.

"Yeah Mark, a million out of work comedians out there and you're telling jokes; keep your day job."

We made small talk for another hour. I hit the sack and slept as if I hadn't slept in days. Almost dying three times in less than a week really takes it out of a person.

By the next afternoon all of the loose ends concerning the Crane case and shooting in Fort Yukon were wrapped up. All of the drugs had been retrieved and a warrant was obtained to search Jeffers' house, but that didn't yield much information though it did result in the recovery of about fifty-thousand in cash and more drugs packaged for an apparent delivery.

I went and personally thanked Fanny Grant and Greg Sharp for all their help. Mark and I caught a flight out of Fort Yukon at about seven p.m. and flew into Fairbanks.

We had a few hours before our flight to Anchorage, so we went to the hospital to visit both Chief Sullivan and Dale Mason.

Mason was seated upright in bed watching a crime investigation show. He smiled when Mark and I entered his room. "You never know what you can learn," he remarked referring to the show he was watching.

Mark shook his good hand. "Thanks for all you did; you're a brave young man."

"Did?" said Dale. "I got shot right off. Thank you for saving my ass!"

We learned that Dale was expected to make a full recovery, a through and through gunshot wound that would heal without problem. I was more worried for all the nurses at the hospital. Dale struck me as a budding ladies man and he knew how to play on their sympathy.

In the Chief's room Claire was seated next to her husband. She stood and gave Mark and me a hug. "Thank you for coming by."

"How is this old son-of-a-gun doing?" I asked.

The Chief looked at me. "Call me old! If Claire wasn't here I would hop out of this bed and show you old," said Chief Sully with a smile.

Chief Sully thanked both Mark and me for everything. "I just don't know how Kyle Jeffers pulled the wool over my eyes."

Mark spoke up. "He fooled a lot of people, not just you. In the end he got what he had coming."

Claire explained that they were returning to Fort Yukon the following morning. With rest, the Chief would be just fine.

Mark and I said our goodbyes and returned to the airport for our flight home.

It was a short forty-five minute flight to Anchorage. We exited the plane and went directly to the luggage carousel to retrieve our bags. As we made our way out to the taxi line I saw Whitney. She was so damn beautiful.

"But how . . ."

"I called her and told her," Mark said before I could even ask the question.

I was astonished. Other than my confession to Chief Sully a couple of days ago, no one knew about Whitney. I suppose a good supervisor should know everything about the people who worked for them.

I rushed up, pulled Whitney into my arms and kissed her. This was perfect.

"There's someone in the car who wants to see you," Whitney smiled.

There in the car was Archie. Now - it really was perfect!

Epilogue

Marcus closed his laptop. He had just finished reading an online newspaper story about an event in Fort Yukon, Alaska. His entire world had just come crashing down. He had so much money and time invested into the perfect avenue and cover to funnel drugs across the Canadian border into the forty-ninth state.

That son-of-a-bitch Jacob Rohn had now cost him literally hundreds of thousands of dollars, hell, perhaps millions. He would have to start all over again grooming his business in the far north. At least he believed he had covered his tracks well enough so that no one would ever be able to link him to the drugs that were recovered or any of the events that had taken place.

Over five years ago Rohn had caused him so much grief and nearly ruined him. His fiancée's sudden death took care of that problem. Who could've ever dreamed Rohn would return to haunt him!

Marcus dialed a Washington State number on his cell phone.

A male voice answered on the other end. "What?"

Marcus skipped the pleasantries and got directly to the point. "We have a huge problem that needs attention."

****

Notes from the Author

Thank you for reading Frozen Lies. I'm quite pleased with my effort and judging by the feedback I've received others are enjoying it as well. Though the story is a work of fiction, I've certainly drawn upon my Alaska State Trooper career to mold the characters and tale itself. There are bits and pieces of many different investigations I worked or was involved with that have found their way into the pages of this book or at least inspired me in some manner.

I worked and lived in Fort Yukon early in my career for a bit over three years. It was tough being the sole trooper for the entire Yukon Flats region which included eight villages but I loved every minute of it. The stories I could tell, actually I've started a book to do just that. Throughout my trooper career I had two other rural assignments. I was stationed in the communities of St. Mary's and Dillingham, of which I suspect both will find their way into my writing.

As I mentioned, there are quite a number of things that I used from my experiences to help mold this story. The greatest contributor from my past would be some of the characters. I modeled many of them after people I knew and worked with over the years but of course their names have been changed. For example, the chief of police in Frozen Lies, Chief Sully, was based on a chief of police I worked with in Fort Yukon. He used the line "what's on your feeble?" often. I know it's an old cliché but I wanted to make a tribute to a man I admired.

There's a second Jake Rohn book nearing completion. Look for 'Deep Lies' to be available early in May of 2013. At least that's my goal. Thanks once again for reading this book and I encourage feedback!

The cover for Frozen Lies is a photo of the Tanana River between Fairbanks and Delta Junction that I took the winter I wrote this book. It's the exact look of the Porcupine River during the winter months. I've travelled the Porcupine River by snowmachine in the heart of a cold Alaska winter. The land is definitely '*frozen*' all around.

I encourage feedback from all who read Frozen Lies.

raquinn@tier1books.com to email me

@BooksByRAQuinn to follow me on twitter

www.facebook.com/booksbyraquinn to like my page on facebook

About The Author

R. A. Quinn currently resides in the small town of North Pole, Alaska with his wonderful family. He had a memorable career as an Alaska State Trooper and worked in almost every corner of the state.

Now he writes, enjoys sports, travels when he can and rides his 2008 Harley Ultra Classic as much as possible.

Other Titles By R. A. Quinn

Frozen Lies (Jacob Rohn book 1)
Deep Lies (Jacob Rohn book 2)
Clear Lies (Jacob Rohn book 3)

These titles are available on Amazon and Barnes & Noble.

www.ingramcontent.com/pod-product-compliance
Lightning Source LLC
LaVergne TN
LVHW091053080826
845145LV00002B/726

* 9 7 8 0 9 8 9 7 3 3 2 1 2 *